the GROWLY books

winter

the GROWLY books

winter

Philip Ulrich

Illustrated by Annie Barnett

Published by Here We Go Productions, LLC,

www.herewegoproductions.com.

ISBN - 978-0-9893852-8-2

Design and Layout by Philip Ulrich.

www.philipulrichdesigns.com.

Illustrations by Annie Barnett, Be Small Studios

www.besmallstudios.com.

Edited by Erin Ulrich

CONTENTS

to our two sweet adventurers ...

prologue:
Through the Telescope

The sound of the Great River thundered all around, seeming to grow even louder as the little figure scrambled up the steep, rocky slope and onto level ground. A strong wind whistled through the treetops, sending swirls of icy spray through the branches of the towering pines.

Clambering up onto a slippery boulder, the figure wiped his eyes with his sleeve and peered through the mist toward the churning rapids. Though he could make out the rapids on the other side of the trees, he could not see anything beyond. He sat there for a moment, stretching his legs out over the moss and wiggling his boots back and forth as he gazed up into the trees. It would be easier to see from up there.

He slid down the other side of the boulder and took off with a jog toward one of the pines. As he came to the foot of the tree, he unclipped his weathered, red backpack, and a moment later, swung himself up onto the nearest branch. It was harder to climb than he expected. The tree was slick from the icy spray, and as he climbed higher, the wind tousled him about, whipping at his jacket and stinging his cheeks.

He took a deep breath and clambered up onto the next branch, his boots scraping on the icy bark as he tried to keep his grip. Not too much further. Just a few branches more and there was a place where he would be able to see out toward the east. Just a few branches more …

A gust of wind came roaring through the forest, making the treetops sway and the icy branches shake. The climber felt his gloves slipping and his boots losing all their grip on the trunk.

All of a sudden he was falling, letting out a panicked cry as he felt himself tumbling through the air. With a crashing thud he smashed into the next branch, sending a shower of tiny icicles down toward the ground far below. As he felt himself begin to fall again, he wrapped one arm around the bough, kicking wildly with his feet as he tried to keep his grip. He could hear the pounding of his heartbeat throbbing in his ears, even above the constant roar of the Great River. That was close!

He hung there precariously for a moment, feet dangling in the air as he clung desperately to the slippery branch. Then with a groan, he pulled himself upward until finally he was standing, with arms wrapped tightly around the trunk of the tree.

As he clung there, a single snowflake swirled down through the branches, twisting past his nose and then off again toward the ground. Winter was still a few months away, but already there were hints of it in the air. He had seen snowflakes a week ago. Just a few, twirling around on a northerly breeze that had come down from the mountains. And yesterday he had awakened with his teeth chattering and his sleeping bag surrounded by frost. Just a few snowflakes, but there would be more … a LOT more.

"Come on," he whispered to himself, "just a little bit higher."

He heaved himself upward, swinging onto the branch above, and then up onto the next. One more …

Standing on the slippery bough, with one arm wrapped around the trunk of the tree, he gazed out through the branches at an astonishing sight. He was up above the mist and spray, looking out across the Great River. Far to the east, beyond the churning waters he could see towering mountains, with icy cliffs soaring up into the clouds. Below them, rolling hills and forests stretched out toward The Precipice. The forests were golden and fiery red, bright with the colors of the fall. The meadows between blazed brilliant and green in the bright mid afternoon sunlight.

Trembling, the climber reached down and pulled a small, folded telescope from his pocket, stretching it out with one end between his teeth and the other in his glove. He put it up to his eye and gazed back out over the water. Far on the other side, he could make out rocky hilltops rising up above the slopes of the riverbanks. Large birds were circling high above the boulders, soaring with slow, steady turns and sometimes diving playfully on the wind. And just below them …

When he saw, it he let out a gasp. Below them flew a bigger pair of wings, with a tiny figure that looked almost like … almost like a bear!

1
Glider Lessons

Growly was running with all his might, stumbling down the grassy slope and trying his best not to trip. "PULL UP!" PULL UP!"

He was shouting as he ran—shouts that were happy cries of laughter, with a little bit of worry mixed in too. Just ahead of him, swerving and jostling on the wind, was a mostly out of control glider with a *mostly* delighted monkey clinging tightly underneath.

"Look Growleeeee!!!!" he cried, dipping down into the long grass and then back up into the air again as he sped on down the hill. He was howling with laughter as he clung to the steering bar. A wide, silly grin stretched from cheek to cheek.

"Growleeeee! I'm flying!!!!"

The glider bumped back into the long grass again, and for a moment the little monkey disappeared from view.

"PUUUUULLLLLL UPPPPP!" Growly howled happily, gasping and laughing as he ran. They were halfway down the hill now, and he could hear the cries and shouts of his friends who were gathered in the meadow at the foot of the steep slope.

The glider shot up into the air again, with Chippy laughing giddily as he swerved back into view. Long strands of grass flapped like streamers from his boots and twirled off behind him as he sped on down the slope.

They were getting close to the bottom now. The little crowd of bears that had been watching at the foot of the hill started to scramble in all directions as Chippy hurtled down into their midst. Ember, who had been watching Chippy's flying lesson with the group, dove desperately to the left as the glider whistled past. There was a brief glimpse of Chippy's grinning face and the bright patterns on the wings as the glider whooshed overhead, followed by another one of Chippy's happy howls of laughter. As she rolled back up onto her feet, Ember could see the glider lift a little higher as it raced on out into the meadow.

"Come on Chippy!" she whispered.

Annily, who had been watching anxiously next Ember, scrambled to her feet and took off at a run after the glider.

"Chippy!!" she was calling. "Chippeeee! Don't you …"

The glider, which had been rising steadily for a moment, suddenly decided to go in a different direction.

"… crash!"

Annily groaned, coming up beside the glider, which had come to a sudden stop after diving back down into the long grass. After a moment, she had freed Chippy from his harness. Soon the two monkeys stood side by side, one shaking her head and smiling affectionately, and the other grinning and pulling a long tuft of grass out of his left boot.

It had been almost a month now since the two monkeys came to Haven, and the bears were still getting used to their presence. It had been a shock to see Growly, appearing so suddenly and strangely after everyone had feared he might be lost. And it had been an even greater shock ... an incredible, astonishing, wonderful shock to see C.J.—the bear who had been missing beyond The Precipice for so many years. But the monkeys? Well, that was the kind of shock the bears didn't really have the exact words to describe.

At first sight, many of the bears had thought they might be quite small bear cubs—very thin ones wearing strange clothes. That would also be a surprise, of course. At closer view, almost every bear quickly realized that these were most certainly NOT quite small, thin cubs in strange clothes. They were something else completely. Growly had tried to explain this, at first, to the astonished crowd that morning at the Cascade River. And he had kept trying to explain it all the way back to Haven as well. C.J. did his best to explain too, but there was so much excitement during the first day back. By the time most of the Cubs of Haven were being tucked into their beds that night and were asking what the little things who came with Growly were, their parents still had no idea. "We're not sure yet..." was whispered in many homes. "We just know they are *not* little cubs in strange clothes."

It was Annily who finally explained about monkeys to the bears of Haven. A feast was set a few days after Growly's return, and Annily gave a wonderful speech about her home in Towerwood and the customs and ways of the monkeys there. She was very fluent in Bear, after studying with C.J. himself, as well as other monkeys who had mastered the Bear language.

After Annily's speech, Chippy sang one of his favorite monkey songs, "Away Beyond the Canyon Wall." It was a song about what might be beyond the cliffs of his homeland, and he sang the third verse doing a handstand, which got all the bears howling with laughter and the Little Cubs doing their best to do handstands too. When things calmed down a little, Growly told about the other monkeys they had encountered in their journeys, and C.J. gave a brief lesson on how to say "hello" in Monkey.

From that day on, Chippy and Annily were constantly invited to dinners and lunches and even breakfasts, not to mention morning, afternoon, and evening teas. It got to be so much that the Mayor had to ask the Haven bears to please let the monkeys rest.

"There is one thing that is of utmost importance now," he had stated importantly in a town meeting, using his important meeting voice. "And though we all love Annily and Chippy, that one thing is not to have them over for a meal. What matters most right now is to find a way to get them home."

And that is what was happening. The Rescue Committee, the engineers, the planners, and the thinkers had been meeting to make a plan. Growly's father, Farren, led many of the meetings. He was the leader of the Rescue Committee, and he had a gift of helping the other bears see new ways of doing things. He asked Ruslan, head of the engineers, to share about what it might take to divert the Cascade River again, so that the tunnel which led down the Precipice could be uncovered.

"It could be possible …" Ruslan had said, his sentence drifting off into a mumble as he put his paw up to his chin. "Hmmm …"

And so the river project began. A big trench would be dug in the Lower Lands, with wheels and gates in place to be able to change the course of the whole river once the dangerous ice chunks were gone in the early spring. There were risks of course, and a big chance that it might not work, but it was a good plan.

"What about flying?" Skye questioned during one of the planning meetings. She was an expert in a glider and longed to fly out over The Precipice, now that she knew there was something beneath the thick clouds. "What if Annily and Chippy could learn to fly, and I could fly down with them?" She smiled an embarrassed smile when she realized if she went with them, she would still need to find a way back up.

It was another option though, and Farren took it seriously. What if Annily and Chippy *could* be taught to fly gliders? With this idea had come another one, which Farren had only shared with Growly, C.J., and a few others. It was going to remain secret for now, while Chippy and Annily continued their lessons.

Growly was the last one to come running up to the group gathered around the glider. Chippy looked up at his friend, his face a little sad. "I'm sorry Growly," he said quietly in Bear. Chippy had learned a lot of the language over the last months, but his accent was still gentle and lilting.

Growly grinned. "As long as you land in long grass, you're going to be just fine, Chippy. We just have to get the flying part right now." He gave Chippy a wink and reached down to grab one wing of the glider. "One more try, Chippington?"

Chippy gave an excited nod as Ember and some of the other bears lifted the glider between them, and they all made their way back toward the hill.

Skye, who had been circling above in her glider earlier, met the group as they made their way up the hill. "You've almost got it Chippy!" she said encouragingly. "Just keep the bar steady and your movements smooth."

"And keep grass out of your boots!" Ash exclaimed with a happy laugh. Ash had always been a close friend of Growly's, and now he had grown close to Chippy, too. The three of them were almost always together.

As they reached the top of the hill again, Growly strapped Chippy into the glider harness, having Gittel check to make sure everything was secure. She was by far the best flight assistant in Haven, though she hated to fly herself.

"Harnesses secure," she said, nodding to the young monkey pilot with a warm smile.

And he was off, running down the slope a short way and then pushing up into the air.

"Come on Chippy," Growly whispered, watching the glider tilt and wobble as it lifted upward.

Chippy *was* getting better, and there were still some weeks to go until the first heavy snows were expected. By spring the monkeys would be ready to fly if the Cascade couldn't be diverted. And that other plan … the one that only a few bears knew about, wouldn't even be needed.

2
A Very Big Change

The main street of Haven was full of bears as Growly and his companions came up the wide path that led into the village from the Little Cliffs. Families were bundled up warmly in fall coats, with hats and caps pulled down tightly over ears. Everyone was heading to the Lookout, for a special meeting had been called. *"A very important announcement, of a very big change."* That's all most bears knew. No one wanted to miss hearing what that important announcement was.

Growly knew. He had been told about a week ago. "So you see, Growly, why you needed to know ahead of time," he had been told. And he had nodded, in wonder, that he understood indeed. Now, as he walked into the village and saw all the bustle and excitement, that feeling of wonder was back with him again.

A large crowd had already gathered at the foot of the Lookout. Cubs were running about, as they almost always did, squeezing between the older bears' legs as they chased after each other. The older bears were all caught up in conversations that seemed to go this way and that without really going anywhere at all. Everyone's minds were on what the announcement would be and what *else* in Haven might be going to change.

Growly and his friends had come directly from the Lower Lands, climbing the narrow path up the Little Cliffs after Chippy and Annily practiced a few more takeoffs in the glider. They had sung Adventure songs on the way home—mostly bear songs, but a few monkey ones as well, which Annily and Chippy had been teaching them over the previous weeks. They had eaten as they hiked and now joined the noisy procession, arriving at the foot of the tower as the last of the Haven families pressed into the bustling crowd.

"Bears of Haven!" A familiar voice boomed down over the gathered crowd. It was the mayor, dressed in his finest coat and hat, his face serious, but with a twinkle in his eyes. He loved speeches and gatherings and special occasions … well … especially speeches.

"Bears … of … Haven," he said again, more slowly this time. The mayor paused on every word in a way that made each one feel very precious and important. He was quiet and thoughtful for a long moment, until suddenly he blinked and shook his head. "And monkeys!" he added suddenly. "Everyone … um …welcome."

Ash looked over at Growly with a puzzled look on his face. The mayor was never lost for words.

"He's ok," Growly whispered, very quietly. He knew what the mayor was about to say.

"Bears and monkeys ... friends ..." The mayor paused again, looking out over the crowd and taking a deep breath.

"For over a thousand years we have lived here on the cliffs of Mount Hegel. Our world has been no bigger than the nearby valleys and forests at the edge of The Precipice. I thought it would never change, that for centuries to come we would keep on imagining what might lie below the clouds as we stood with our Cubs at the edge of The Precipice. For centuries it has been the end of our world. Now we know it is just the beginning.

"C.J. has returned," he continued, and now there were tears in the corners of his eyes, "after ... after all these years ... and ... and monkeys!" The mayors voice was quivering and raspy, but it carried out clearly over the hushed crowd. The mayor was silent for a long moment, and then said again, still raspy and shaking, but louder and with a voice full of wonder, "*Monkeys!*"

He looked out over the crowd, taking in another long, deep breath.

"Bears of Haven," he finally said, a gentle smile beginning to show at the corners of his mouth. "These are not ordinary times." As he spoke, other bears came out onto the raised area next to him. It was the Elder Bears of the Council. They stretched out in a line on either side of the mayor as he continued.

"Since the arrival of C.J., Growly, Annily, and Chippy, the Council has been meeting to discuss what their arrival means to the bears of Haven. We have spoken with them all, on many occasions. C.J., who stands here with us now as a full member of the Council, has advised us and taught us and helped us to see a world beyond our own. There is much to be told in the coming days, but for tonight, what I want to tell you is this. It has been an honor to be your mayor, but a brand new role is beginning for me now."

There were loud gasps and a few cries throughout the crowd. Then, a stunned silence settled back over the gathered bears. A wide smile was on the mayor's face now though, and as he spoke again, there was true happiness in his voice.

"Friends," his voice was warm as it boomed out. "Let me reassure you. If there is an occasion to be announced ... I will announce it! If there is tradition to be cherished ... I will hold onto it with both paws! And my feet!" There was a roar of laughter from the crowd. "An Adventure song to be sung ... I will lead it with all my heart." He had a wide, happy grin now, and a sparkle in his eyes. "And if there is a speech to be made ... well ... I will try not to be shy!" There was another roar of laughter from the crowd, which carried on until the mayor waved his arms and continued.

"These are *not* ordinary times ... no. They are extraordinary! A lost bear can return! A Young Bear can cross an Ocean! ... Monkeys! Our Little Cubs will know about monkeys. Life will never be the same here again."

The mayor looked out over the faces of his friends for a long, quiet moment. "But we will still have our stories, our songs and traditions, and our speeches and ceremonies. It is what I do best," he added with a wink. "And someone has to remember the words of 'The Ode to Bartholomew the Brown.' All twenty-three verses! I think I'm the only one who knows."

The bears let out another roar of laughter. It was true. Very few of them knew more that just a few lines. It really *was* a terrible song.

"These extraordinary times will require new things from all of us and a mayor who does much more than any mayor before." The mayor paused again for a moment, stretching an arm out towards the lookout as he continued. "We have chosen Farren to be the new mayor, though we may need to find a new name for the role he will fill."

There was a moment of silence as the news sunk in and then a roar of approval as Farren stepped out of the shadows into view next to the mayor. Growly's father was the leader of the Rescue Committee and was well loved in the village. He had led a rescue for two lost bears in a recent storm and had coordinated the search for Growly when it was discovered he was missing. Finding a way home for Annily and Chippy was going to require clear thinking and brave decisions, and Farren was known for both.

Chippy looked up at Growly with a grin, and Ash nudged him in the elbow.

Growly was beaming with pride. He knew without a doubt his father would lead Haven well.

As Farren stood with the mayor and the Elder Bears, Growly's mother, Edolie, stepped up next to her husband, taking his paw in hers.

"And now," said the mayor, "there is only one more thing left to do."

Turning toward Farren, he took off his tall hat and handed it to C.J., who was standing by his side. With a slight bow, the mayor lifted off the large medallion which hung around his neck, and placed it gently over Farren's head.

"You will lead us well," the mayor said softly, though he wasn't really the mayor any more. "An extraordinary bear for extraordinary times," he whispered, patting Farren affectionately on the shoulder.

The mayor turned back to the crowd, and was about to finish his speech and announce Farren as the official new mayor when there was a sudden, desperate cry from above. It was Pepper, Ruslan's daughter. She had been on watch duty at the top of the Lookout during the ceremony, and now she waved frantically toward the west, before disappearing back into the tower door again.

There was confusion everywhere, a loud babble of conversation as to what it might be that Pepper had seen. The Elder Bears gathered around Farren and the mayor, deep in conversation while watching the entryway at the base of the Lookout. It wasn't long until Pepper reappeared, flinging the large door wide, running over to the the Elders, and speaking earnestly as she pointed toward the west. As she spoke, C.J. and a few of the others raced off toward the tower, followed closely by Farren and Edolie.

Growly and Ember didn't have any idea what was going on, and Ash shrugged his shoulders and shook his head. It wasn't long though till Farren appeared again at the foot of the Lookout, running out through the large doorway to come and address the crowd.

"Friends," he said finally, his voice calm and steady, "we are in no danger. But Heflin's Reach is covered with fire!"

3
Heflin's Reach

There was a sudden rush of activity. Parents hurried about, anxiously gathering their Little Cubs with the help of those nearby. Bears not chasing after Cubs began to gather with their assigned groups, as was always the case in times of emergency. Was this an emergency? No one at all was sure. Still, gathering with your group seemed the best thing to do. The engineers met at the far end of the rock on which the Lookout was built. The pilots gathered a little further up the hill which led toward Glider Leap, and the Rescue Committee assembled around Farren, who was still standing out in front of the Lookout with C.J. and Merridy and some of the Elders.

"Fires!" Farren gasped, "all over the island. Pepper said they seemed to spring up out of nowhere. There is no lightning about." Farren paused and put his paw up to his chin, looking down at the ground, and then off toward the west before he continued.

"I had a quick look through one of the telescopes. You know how hard it is to see the island from here. Now with all the smoke and flame, it was hard to see much at all." He paused again, putting both paws together under his nose and looking off into the distance, deep in thought. Growly and the other bears of the Rescue Committee waited quietly. This was how Farren came up with his plans. It just took a little patience and waiting.

"Telescopes!" he exclaimed suddenly. Farren looked up at the bears gathered around him. "I believe we must find out more about these fires, if we possibly can." Turning to C.J., Growly, and Chippy, he continued. "You all saw rivers of fire in your travels. What if these fires were something like that? Heflin's Reach may be far out in the waters of the Great River, but what if fires like those could happen here too? We must find out more if we possibly can."

There was no disagreement from C.J. or the Elder Bears, and Growly and Chippy looked at each other with a shiver. They hadn't liked the rivers of fire at all!

"All four of the big telescopes for now," Farren continued, after seeing the Elder Bears nod in agreement. "Two bears carrying at a time. We will take turns through the night until we reach the edge of the Great River." He motioned to eight of the strongest bears, who ran off immediately, up into the Lookout.

"We will need food and other supplies, enough for a week, and as many other small telescopes as can be carried. I will talk to the engineers about building wooden towers if needed. For shelters, we will need sleeping bags and tents." Growly looked up at a swirling flake of snow that had just twirled around the Lookout on an icy breeze coming down from the mountains. Farren saw it too.

"Dress warm," he said seriously. "Full winter coats and pants. We are going to be sleeping out in the cold."

Heflin's Reach was a long, thin island, far out in the churning, rumbling rapids of the Great River. It was named, of course, after Hegel's close friend, Heflin, who had traveled on the desperate march from their home in the west over a thousand years ago. Heflin, Janika, and many of the other bears were separated from Hegel at the place where the Great River now thundered. Heflin's Reach was the last place those bears had been seen, though Hegel wrote later he was sure they made it back to the other side.

Growly had often wondered what it might be like out on the island. There were two small forests and a long, wide, grassy area dotted with enormous boulders. On a clear day when the spray from the Great Falls wasn't too heavy, you could see a lot of it through a telescope. There were many areas though, hidden in the low places and woods and shadows, which no bear in Haven had ever seen. As Growly rushed into his home, grabbing his rescue pack, tent, and winter clothes, he hoped maybe these strange fires might reveal something new.

Chippy was right behind him as they raced back out into the street. He had been staying with Growly since they arrived, sleeping on an extra bed Ash had delivered from his father's workshop.

The two friends ran down to the end of the village, where a large group of bears was gathering at the edge of the Little Cliffs. It wasn't just the Rescue Committee either. There was a large group of engineers, and even many of the bakers and chefs. The four large telescopes from the Lookout were laid out on the ground with long shoulder harnesses to make the carrying easier.

"All right then," Farren called, as the last of the group came jogging down the street with their packs. "Bears with lamps in front of every telescope and also leading groups of six. We switch carriers at the foot of the cliffs. Are we ready?"

There were some shouts and nods and yeses, but it was not really a question. Everyone was eager to get to the Great River to find out what was happening on Heflin's Reach.

"Do you think it *is* rivers of fire, Growly?" Chippy whispered shakily as they made their way along the zigzagging path that led down the Little Cliffs.

Growly could see Chippy was uneasy, a lot like the uneasy feeling that he was feeling too.

Growly thought for a moment. Rivers of fire were a *very* strange thing, and a very hard thing for a bear to understand. But there was something about this that just didn't make sense. He just couldn't quite put his paw on what I was.

They would hike through the night and the following morning, out across the Lower Lands and then into a small range of hills. Just beyond these hills, they would come to the Banks, a thin stretch of land that ran along the edge of the Great River. It was here that they would make camp and set up the telescopes.

As they hiked through the night, Ember and Skye led the group in a wide range of bear hiking songs. They had a way singing with such exuberance that, even though the hiking was difficult, the miles rushed by and everyone's moods were lightened a little. Gittel sang some cooking songs, and Ash joined right in with her. He didn't know much about cooking, but he knew a lot about food. Especially about eating it! And though singing about it wasn't quite as good as *eating* it to him, food singing was still very, very good.

The morning came, frosty and golden over The Precipice, slowly lighting up the Lower Lands as the group raced across the meadows. By midmorning, they had reached the low hills, with the light of the sun now bright, high up in the mountains. There was smoke here. Everyone could smell it, and a thick, dark plume of it rose high into the air on the other side of the ridge. Though they were all tired, the group quickened their pace, pushing their way up the slopes with all of their strength. As they reached the top, Growly gasped, as did many of the other bears when they looked across the Great River.

Out amongst the churning, swirling, thundering rapids, in the middle of the sheets of mist and spray blowing up from the Great Falls, Heflin's Reach was covered in fire. Many fires. Growly could see them blazing all over the island.

"The telescopes!" Farren called loudly, pointing toward a grassy rise on the top of the hill. "We will set up two here, with two more by those boulders down there closer to the river."

It was a very chilly day, and even in the rush of activity, Growly had to pull his coat tighter against the icy wind. The air near the river was damp with sleet and icy spray.

One of the telescopes was almost ready, resting on a portable stand that had been carried down from Haven. There was a large group of bears heading down toward the river—Ember and Annily and many from the Rescue Committee. Growly fumbled with the straps on the second telescope, blowing on his paws for a moment to keep them warm. In a moment, they had the second telescope ready, and Growly put his face up to the eyepiece to make sure everything was still in focus. It would just take a moment to adjust all the gauges and …

Growly let out a sudden cry of surprise, stumbling back from the telescope for a moment in shock.

"Growly! What is it?" Chippy whispered urgently.

"I … It's …" Growly didn't know what to say. It couldn't be! He had to look again. He put his eye back up to the telescope, looking out toward the island through the spray and the smoke. There were fires on the island, many of them, stretching from one end of the island to the other. And in between the fires was a desperately waving figure. A figure that looked a lot like … a bear!

4
Flags & Symbols

I t is a bear. There is no doubt about it. But that flag ..." C.J. said, looking away from the eyepiece and nodding in assurance to those around him.

All four telescopes were set up now, spread out along the hilltop where all the bears now gathered. They were talking excitedly, taking turns looking out through the large telescopes and through smaller ones of their own.

The figure on the island was a Young Bear. Or maybe even an older Cub. He was smaller than Growly, dressed in boots, thick pants, and a worn and weathered coat. He was standing now on the closest side of the island, waving a large flag that looked like it might have been made out of a sheet. Every so often he would jam the pole of the flag between some rocks and take out his telescope, looking out across the waters to the hilltop where everyone was gathered.

He had seen them. That was for certain. After gazing through his telescope for a while, he would lay it down beside him, waving his arms wildly before taking up his flag once again. The flag was white and ragged at the ends, and a strange, unfamiliar symbol was scrawled across the middle.

"Have you seen it before?" Farren asked quietly, as C.J. stepped away from one of the large telescopes looking puzzled.

"No, not in anything I have read. Merridy?" C.J. looked to his wife, the librarian, wondering if she might have seen the symbol in one of the library books.

Merridy shook her head. "All signs and symbols are categorized in the library index. I go over it every year. That symbol ..." she nodded out toward the island, "... I have never seen that one."

C.J. was quiet for a moment, thinking back on all the signs and symbols he had seen over the years, trying to remember what the one on the strange bear's flag could possibly mean. Suddenly, his face lit up with an idea. "Of course!" he exclaimed. It was mostly to himself, but he looked at Merridy with excitement in his eyes. "We need to make a flag of our own, and I think I know what needs to be written on it!"

There was a rush of activity. Skye collected a large sheet from one of the packs, while C.J. and Merridy talked quietly together, nodding in agreement.

The Young Bears, along with Annily and Chippy, already had a fire going. They would need charcoal to draw the markings on the flag. "And to cook lunch," Ash added, which made Gittel smile. Ash made a large paint brush from some thick, dry grass found down by the river. Soon a large flag was ready, with an old, familiar marking on its side.

"The mark of Hegel!" Growly whispered in wonder, turning to Chippy to explain. "That is the marking the bears used in the olden days. It's in the old language. And that word underneath … every Cub learns it: *Whistiglen*—the name of the old Bear language, and also the name of their old home in the west. Cubs in Haven learn many Whistiglen words. Perhaps the bear on that island knows some too."

The flag was big, and it took four bears to lift it up and set it in place amongst a large pile of rocks. Two bears climbed up on a makeshift stand, stretching the flag out so it wouldn't flap in the wind. Looking through the telescope, Growly could see the bear on the island pause for a moment and then lay down the flag he had been waving. Reaching down into the grass beside him, the bear picked up his telescope again, putting it to his eye and gazing up toward the hilltop.

The bear stood there for a long time, hardly moving at all until, suddenly, he lifted his telescope up into the air, waving his other arm wildly and nodding. As Growly watched, the bear took his flag, laying it down on the ground while he went to get cooled charcoal from one of the fires. He crushed and mixed and crushed some more, and then set about working on the flag again with a brush. Growly couldn't see what was being written. Even through the large telescope it was hard to make out much of what was happening on the island.

"Look!" C.J. exclaimed. He had been watching through one of the other large telescopes, waiting to see if the bear on the island understood. "Merridy! See if you can tell!"

Growly was watching the bear lift up his flag, which now looked like a banner, with a pole on either side. There were writings on it that almost looked familiar … almost. Growly stepped back from the telescope, letting Merridy climb up to peer through the eyepiece. "Oh C.J. It's in *Whistiglen!* The letters look a little different, but it *is* Whistiglen!

"Yes!" C.J. replied excitedly. It's the mark of Hegel, and that word underneath—I think it means something like … village?"

"Or many bears!" Merridy shouted excitedly. "It's used that way in Hegel's eighth poem in *Early Writings* where …" Merridy stopped suddenly and looked around at everyone with a slightly embarrassed smile. "Where librarians sometimes get a little carried away," she added, her smile turning to a grin before she looked back into the telescope. "That word … the last two letters are quite strange, but I'm pretty sure that's what it says."

"Many bears?" C.J. was puzzled. He looked over at Merridy and around at everyone again. "Perhaps there are more? But where?"

Farren, who was standing not far from C.J., called out to the bears at the other two telescopes. "Keep looking for others!" His voice didn't sound very sure though.

"The mark of Hegel!" Ember's excited voice almost made Growly jump in surprise. "Mama! Don't you remember what you taught us about the mark of Hegel?"

Merridy, who was still trying to figure out if the word really meant *village* or *many bears* looked up at her daughter in confusion for a moment. "The mark of Hegel?"

"Yes Mama. In *Little Cubs History* at the library. You taught us about the mark of Hegel. As the bears of his time were traveling east, when someone was in danger they would use the mark of Hegel to call for …"

"Rescue!" Merridy gasped.

"Rescue! Many bears!" C.J. added. He had come over from his telescope. "Many bears," he repeated. "Perhaps a whole village."

Growly's mind was racing. A whole village? On Heflin's Reach? There were parts of the island that had never been seen, but how could that be possible?

The bear on the island was standing beside his banner, watching through his telescope to see what would happen next.

"Another sheet!" Farren called suddenly, looking around as he tried to figure out the next thing to do. "The mark of Hegel!" he said, looking seriously at C.J. and Merridy, and then slowly around at the whole group. "Write the mark of Hegel! Rescue! Let him

know that help is coming. Though right now I don't
know exactly what it is."

It wasn't long till the second flag was flying,
stretched out up on the hilltop, larger than the first.
The bear on the island waved joyfully when he saw it
and then sat down by one of the fires to keep warm
from the icy river winds. Growly watched him through
the telescope. He looked tired and dirty, but his
movements now seemed full of hope.

The bears on the hillside were already busy.
Chippy and Annily were with the engineers. Chippy
was an expert inventor; Growly had seen that himself.
Annily was very gifted too. They were looking over
plans to develop some kind of walkway. Perhaps a
raised bridge of some sort. Towers?

Farren was meeting with Skye, Ember, Growly,
and many of the other pilots. The winds over the
Great River were treacherous. But so were the winds
out over The Precipice. The island was far out in the
Great River, but surely there must be a way. There had
to be a way.

"Look!" cried a young bear's voice suddenly,
startling the two groups deep in discussion. It was
Palavi, one of the bears who had been preparing food
at the fire. She seemed to be pointing out toward the
island.

As Growly looked though, he noticed she wasn't
pointing to the island but the sky up above. Whistling
down through the smoky spray were eagles, one after
the other, tilting and turning on the wind as they raced

above the rapids. Down they sped, and as they reached the island they shot through the trees, circling out around the fires as they called out to the startled bear below.

"Goldentail!" Ember cried, pointing toward the island. "It's Goldentail and the eagles from the cliffs."

5
Eagles & Bears

Eagles and bears had lived together for over a thousand years, sharing the cliffs and peaks of the mountains stretching out beyond Mt. Hegel. Though no eagle had ever flown down into Haven, they enjoyed each other's company, and Goldentail had even helped the bears on more than one occasion. Ember put her short telescope up to her eye again, nodding in excitement as she saw the familiar streak of gold amongst the brown and white feathers.

The eagles were circling around the astonished bear on the island, darting through the plumes of smoke as they let out their shrieking cries. Ember could see the bear had his paws up over his head. It was obvious, even through a telescope, that the Young Bear on the island was very afraid.

Goldentail, who had led the other eagles in over the river, now swooped down low, twisted around one of the blazing fires, and came to a sudden, skillful landing a short distance from the bear. As he landed, Goldentail bowed low to the ground, spreading his wings out wide to show that he meant the bear no harm. It was a well know sign that the eagles had used back when they had first encountered the bears of Haven.

The bear on the island had not seen it before though. Ember was certain of that. As she watched through the telescope, she saw him tumble back in alarm, scrambling off toward the river before diving behind a large outcrop of rock.

"He doesn't understand," Growly called. He was watching through a small telescope too, as were Ash and Chippy and most of the others. "The eagles want to help, I think. Though I can't imagine how."

"Look!" Ember cried. Goldentail was in the air again, flying up above the island to join the other eagles circling higher and higher. "They are coming this way!"

Goldentail was in the lead, swooping and turning through the treacherous gusts and swirling winds, which howled above the river. The other eagles were right behind him, diving lower as they came to the Banks, then swooping powerfully up the hillside and landing near the gathered bears. Ember was already running to meet them. She had always loved the eagles and flew with them in her glider whenever she could. Goldentail let out a happy call as he saw Ember bowing, and he stretched out his wings and bowed in return.

"Goldentail!" Ember said breathlessly, wishing she knew a few words in Eagle or even just a few words in …

"Papa!" Ember exclaimed, turning back to C.J. who was with the other bears. "Papa, you could speak with Tully. Do you think an eagle might understand?"

C.J. was quiet for a moment, thinking back on years past. He had traveled with a little blue and red bird named Tully, and they had found a way to communicate: A little bit of Bear language, and a little bit of Bird. He had never tried Eagle though. They had a language all their own.

"It's worth a try," C.J. said. "It feels like so long since I talked with Tully, though it has only been a month. I think it will be wonderful to speak a little Bird again."

"This bird is not little at all!" Ember said, giving C.J. a loving grin. "Now, here's what I was thinking." She leaned close and spoke quietly to the older bear for a moment, as he nodded and asked a few questions in return. Then C.J. waved for Farren to come over to hear Ember's idea.

Farren nodded as he listened, questioning both C.J. and Ember before calling out to Growly.

"We'll need a large sheet of paper, Growly, and a brush and pens. Ember has had an idea, and I think it might be our best chance. Also, we will need as much rope as can be gathered," Farren continued. "Lay out the coils over there. This will all make a lot more sense to you soon."

Growly ran off to find the paper and pens, calling out to other bears for help as he went. Soon there were coils of rope laid out along the hilltop, and C.J. and Merridy were hard at work with the brushes, pens, and paper.

They were writing out words in the old Bear language—the language that was used back in the times of Hegel. "We must keep the sentences simple," Merridy instructed, and C.J. nodded in agreement as he thought of easier words to use.

There were also drawings sketched on smaller sheets of paper—drawings made by Chippy and the engineers. Many of the sheets were instructions for tying special knots: slipknots and square knots and harness knots as well. There was no knowing how much the bear on the island knew, so there must be instructions to make sure he was safe. As safe as he *could* be, Growly thought to himself with a shiver. Ember's plan was the best chance, but it was still dangerous and very unsure. If many bears needed rescue though, it had to be tried.

Ember was at work on another large piece of paper, sketching and drawing with pencil and pen. As she finished, she showed it to Farren, Chippy, and some of the engineers, who all nodded in approval. "I'm going to give it a try Growly," she said with a nervous smile. "Goldentail and the eagles have been watching all this time."

It was true. The large eagle had been standing a short distance away, surrounded by the others who had flown down with him from the mountains.

"Ready, Papa?" Ember asked, and C.J. nodded.

The two of them walked slowly toward the eagles, taking careful, steady steps so as not to alarm the enormous birds. As they came closer, Goldentail stretched his wings wide again, bowing low in a sign of welcome. Ember and C.J. bowed gently too, spreading their arms out as they did so. As they came closer, Ember stretched out the large drawing she had been working on, laying it on the ground in front of Goldentail for the eagle to see. It was then that C.J. let out a quiet whistle, a strange, lilting trill followed by three louder calls.

It felt strange for the Elder Bear to be making those sounds once more. He had only ever talked like that with one other bird—Tully. The little blue and red bird had been gone for over a month now, back on the the long journey to the Monkey Island—to his family.

Goldentail looked up at C.J. suddenly, tilting his head first to one side, and then slowly to the other. It was obvious he was startled, but had he understood? This time C.J. whistled a loud, long call, which got higher at the end and then sunk down into silence.

Goldentail took a startled step backwards, pausing for a moment and blinking in surprise.

"Look!" Merridy whispered softly in Growly's ear. "See how carefully he is looking at C.J., and tilting his head?"

Growly nodded. He had listened before, fascinated, as C.J. had taught on the languages of birds. Most types of birds have their very own languages. A duck doesn't speak sparrow, and a crow doesn't speak swan. But there are some simple words that are understood by all. C.J wasn't sure about eagles though. Eagles had always been very hard to get to know.

Goldentail didn't reply, but he stepped forward again, looking down carefully at the drawing laid out on the ground. He studied it for a long time, glancing up at Ember, and then out toward the island in the middle of the Great River.

After a moment, Goldentail took the edge of the

drawing in his beak, dragging it carefully across the grass to where the other eagles were gathered. He spoke to them as they crowded in closely, in loud cries and calls that sounded familiar to the bears, but also in quiet, gentle sounds that didn't seem like Eagle at all.

Ember watched carefully as they talked, trying to understand by their sounds and their movements what they might finally decide. It *was* a desperate plan. There was a lot that could go wrong, and not just for the bear on the island. Ember's plan was very dangerous for the eagles too.

Suddenly, one of the eagles let out a loud cry, taking a few steps away from the group before it flapped up into the air. The eagle shot up higher and higher, racing out over the Lower Lands and off toward the mountains. Other eagles were taking off now too.

Ember felt her hear sink. Without the help of the eagles, how could they possibly rescue that bear?

"They're all leaving," Growly groaned, and some of the other bears sat down on the soft grass, watching the eagles get smaller and smaller as they flew toward the mountains.

Only Goldentail remained. He stood there for a long time in front of Ember's drawing, looking carefully at her with a constant, steady, gaze. She knelt down on the soft grass, feeling sadder and sadder as the time went by.

"It is far too dangerous," Ember said softly at last.

"You all have families, and the Great River is so wild. I don't blame you at all. I …"

"Eagles!" someone cried. It was Ash, who was looking through one of the large telescopes at the cliffs and mountains near Haven. "It's more—more eagles, and they are coming right this way!"

6
Rivers & Ropes

There were many more of them this time—a long line of eagles swooping down into the Lower Lands. There were others coming from the cliffs too. Growly could see them through the eyepiece of the telescope, tiny specks at first, flying out around Mount Hegel and southward over the Banks.

Ember jumped excitedly to her feet, looking over at Goldentail in delight. "Thank you!" she breathed.

"They are coming!" Farren exclaimed happily. "You all know what to do."

Bears were on their feet, grabbing coils of rope and stretching them out across the hillside. Others were measuring distances and tying knots. Goldentail, who had been watching from a distance, flew up to meet the first of the eagles returning from the mountains. They circled there high above the bears, as more and more eagles arrived, calling out to each other as they watched the activity below.

The bears had stretched out two long, thick ropes, tying many knots out toward the ends. The two ropes were joined in the middle, with long straps and a harness about the size of a bear.

"An eagle couldn't carry a Young Bear," Ember had told Growly, "but perhaps many eagles could. That's what I drew on the paper: many eagles all lifting those ropes. And now, look at them coming! Oh Growly, look at them all!"

The eagles were continuing to come, circling overhead as they arrived and then slowly descending to land with the others gathered farther along the crest of the hill. There were many more than were needed, at least as far as Ember had imagined, but it seemed every eagle in the area wanted to see what was going on.

C.J. and Merridy had been gathering the drawings of the knots, and were now working on a simple note, written in the old Bear language.

As Growly looked down at the note, he could see the familiar inscription of the mark of Hegel—*rescue*.

Underneath were two words, *birds* and *friends*, with a simple sketch of an eagle and bear side by side. Under that, Merridy had written a longer message, in the common language that the bears of Haven used now.

"I have written him about Ember's plan, the eagles, and what he should do," Merridy said, looking up at Growly with a smile. "It seems he knows at least a little of *Old Bear*, perhaps he understands far more in *New*."

The bear had been watching them from the island

through his telescope. He had found a place on a large boulder by the edge of the river.

"He has hardly looked away for the last hour," Ash told them. "Now that the smoke is clearing, I can see him better across the rapids."

It was true. The fires on the island were dying down, battered by the swirling flurries of snow and sheets of icy spray.

"He is looking at the eagles, I think. He has been watching them for a while."

Ash was thoughtful for a moment, then called out to Ember, trying to keep his voice low so as not to startle the gathered birds. "Ember!" he called. "He is looking at the eagles. Show him that he doesn't need to be afraid."

Ember nodded, walking slowly over to the eagles, stretching out her arms and bowing with a wide smile spread across her face.

"He is afraid," she said softly. "The bear upon the island. He is in trouble, and I think he has never seen birds like you. Will you let me touch your feathers, Goldentail, to show him he doesn't need to be afraid?"

Ember knew the eagle didn't understand her words, but as she slowly lifted a trembling paw, the magnificent bird didn't move. Ember carefully took another step closer, stretching her arm out fully until her paw was right beside his shoulder. Goldentail was standing perfectly still, and every bear (and monkey) on the hilltop was now watching, hardly daring to breathe. Ember gently laid her shaking paw on the eagle's soft feathers, leaving it there for a moment as she let out her breath. It was then that the eagle did something quite astonishing. He lifted one powerful wing, and brushed his long, soft feathers down her cheek.

Ash, who was looking through his telescope, whispered excitedly. "He's on his feet! The bear on the island saw it all, and now he is on his feet."

Growly looked through his own telescope and could see the bear standing on the enormous boulder, his telescope pointed toward Ember and the eagles on the hill.

"The ropes," Farren called. At first his voice was not much more than a whisper, not wanting to startle the eagles. "Ember, do you think they are ready?"

Ember turned back to Goldentail. She was beaming happily at the touch from her friend. Though they had never once spoken, she had grown to love this wonderful bird. She pointed toward the ropes and showed the picture she had drawn once again. "Are you ready, Goldentail?"

Goldentail let out a loud call, and suddenly the other eagles swooped down to take the ropes in their strong talons. Some lifted the harness, and others flapped up into the air, circling above the hilltop.

It was Goldentail who would carry the rolled up papers. Ember tied a string around them and then carefully laid them down in front of the eagle. "I'll see you soon my friend," she said softly. "Oh, please be careful!"

The eagles now had the ropes and harness stretched out between them as they lifted high above the hilltop and then on toward the river. As they flew out over the water, they were jostled this way and that by the powerful winds that blew up from the Great Falls, which plunged over The Precipice. Sheets of stinging, icy spray swirled around above the river too, but the eagles pressed on.

Soon they had reached the island, coming to a landing in a small clearing not far from the stranded bear. Growly watched through one of the large telescopes as the eagles landed. They came in two by two, stretching out the ropes in the grass.

The bear watched cautiously from the boulder, and even though Growly was a long way away, he could see the small figure leaning forward a little, hoping to see what the eagles were doing.

Goldentail was coming close now. Growly took his eye from the telescope and made sure Ember was watching. She was on the next large telescope, hardly breathing as the large eagle swooped in.

Goldentail descended gracefully around the large boulder in a wide, gentle circle until he came to a soft landing in the grass in front of the bear. The eagle had let go of the rolled papers he had been carrying, and now he bowed low to the watching bear, spreading his wings wide and nudging the papers forward with his beak. Then he slowly moved backward, step by step away from the boulder.

There was no movement for a moment. The bear

on the rock gazed down at the rolled up papers. He then looked back out across the river, to where the bears watched breathlessly from the hilltop. Nothing happened for a long moment, but then, all at once, as if he had suddenly made up his mind, the bear slid down the side of the boulder and ran to the papers laying rolled up in the grass.

The eagles, who had been gathered near the outstretched ropes, now began to move further away into the clearing, led by Goldentail, who was watching the young bear carefully. The bear studied the papers while scratching nervously behind his ear.

He stood still for a long time, glancing over at the eagles, then back down at the ropes. His shoulders looked tired and hunched, at least as far as Growly could tell through the telescope. As if he wanted to give up and go back home. As if he wanted to cry.

"Come on ..." Growly whispered. He knew how that hopeless feeling felt. "Please."

Looking out across the river one last time, the bear suddenly turned, stepping away from the rope and the eagles, and walking tiredly out of sight behind the boulder.

Growly felt his heart sink, and he heard Ember groan.

"It was a good plan Ember," Growly said with a kind smile. There were *yeses* and nods of agreement from the other bears around them.

"So close!" Farren whispered. "Why…?"

"His backpack!" Chippy cried suddenly, pointing with excitement toward the island.

The bear had come back out from behind the boulder with a red backpack and was headed toward the ropes.

7
Breckin's Tale

There was a cheer from the bears on the hill, and Farren threw his arm around Growly's shoulder, raising his other paw excitedly in the air.

"He's putting on the harness!" Ember cried. "And look! Now he is bowing!"

Growly could see it all through his telescope. The bear had the harness strapped firmly around him, and now, with arms stretched wide, he bowed to the eagles. Goldentail bowed too. Then, opening his beak with a cry Growly could only see through the telescope, the large eagle signaled to the others. Eagles spread out along the ropes, each at one of the knots which the bears had tied earlier. Others flew up into the air above the island, circling and ready for when they would be needed. Two eagles lifted the bear's backpack, stretched out between them as they made their way out across the river.

With the eagles in place along the ropes, Goldentail let out another call, and the ropes were lifted, higher and higher into the air. "Come on!" Ember whispered, and Growly nodded his head, so focused on what was happening that he didn't even notice he was holding his breath.

The ropes were stretched out now, and the bear was running slowly through the long grass as the eagles gathered speed. They were working hard, flapping with all the strength of their powerful wings to lift the bear and to push against the howling winds.

"Come on!" Ember gasped again. The bear was coming closer and closer to the edge of the island, and the eagles still were fighting to lift.

The bear pushed himself off the ground with a leap to see if he could help the eagles. For a moment he lifted high into the air, but then came drifting down again, just a short distance from the island's edge.

The eagles were straining with all their might, and others were swooping in, searching for any place on the rope where they could take hold. Growly could see the dismay on the bear's face through the telescope. He was running out of land and he knew it. With one last push, he leaped up into the air again, soaring out above the water as the island fell behind. He was lifted higher for a moment, swirling and twisting on the ropes in the perilous winds.

"He's coming down again!" Ember cried, and it looked like it was true, though it was hard to tell in all the twirling sleet and spray.

The eagles were keeping him above the waters, but as Growly watched, he wasn't sure they could keep him there for long. Suddenly a dark shape appeared through the spray, swooping in behind the dangling bear as it spread its wings out wide.

"Goldentail!" Ember cried.

The large eagle wrapped his claws around the harness, pushing his powerful wings upward as the bear began to lift. Higher and higher they went, until finally they were speeding above the roaring waters, cutting through the wind as they made their way toward land.

As the eagles reached the river's edge, the bears on the hill let out a mighty cheer, hugging each other and dancing around in celebration and relief. The eagles were speeding over the Banks now, swapping out as they went along to give the tired ones some rest. It wasn't long until their calls could be heard on the wind, and then just a little while longer till they came soaring up over the hilltop with the bear dangling precariously underneath.

Farren and the others around him rushed to help as the ropes came closer to the ground, releasing the the bear quickly from the harness so he could sit down gently on the soft grass. He was shaking all over, and for a long moment he didn't say anything.

He was smaller than Growly had thought he would be from watching through the telescope. Now that he could see the bear more closely, Growly realized with shock that he probably wasn't a Young Bear at all. "You're a Cub!" Growly stammered in surprise, kneeling down in front of the trembling bear, and looking at him in wonder.

The bear nodded shakily, taking a long, deep breath before he spoke.

"I … I'm Breckin. I will be a Young Bear soon though. After summer next."

"A Cub!" C.J. said in astonishment. "A Cub on Heflin's Reach!"

"Help me … please!" Breckin whispered earnestly, looking anxiously up at C.J. and then around at the gathered bears.

Merridy knelt next to Growly and put her paw gently on the trembling Cub's shoulder.

"There, there," she said warmly, giving him a reassuring smile. "Catch your breath for a moment and have a sip of tea. You look like you're half frozen, and that flight with the eagles would get any bear's heart pounding. "

Breckin nodded thankfully, drawing in another deep breath and gratefully accepting the steaming mug of tea, which had been brought to him by Gittel. "I've got pancakes too, whenever you'd like some," she added with a grin.

Breckin's eyes lit up, and he smiled, a happy, hungry Cub grin, though his paws were still shaking.

Gittel was back in a few moments, carrying a plate of fresh pancakes, which had been cooking on the fire. Breckin didn't even wait for syrup. He took the pancakes in his paw, one by one, stuffing them down hungrily between gulps of tea.

"I'm sorry for my manners," he mumbled between bites and sips. "It has been so long since I had a good meal like this."

No one minded at all.

"Ash eats like this all the time when it comes to

pancakes!" Gittel joked. That got everyone roaring with laughter. Especially Ash.

"Now," Merridy said softly. "Whenever you are ready, tell us all you can."

Wiping a pancake crumb from the corner of his mouth, Breckin began his story.

"We weren't ready for it at all. None of us. One night we went to bed as usual, and early the next morning we awoke to the sound of the alarm bells and horns. Water was everywhere, rumbling and roaring through our village, with half of the surrounding forests already underwater. Thankfully, we made it to higher ground. All of us eventually. Most of our supplies were washed away though. Our village of Arborstone was left half sunken, far from the shore in the Salington Sea. Winter would soon be coming, and we had lost our village and our food."

Breckin stopped for a moment to quickly eat another pancake with a gulp of tea.

"We decided to break into teams of four, everyone who could travel. Some to forage for food and others to search for help. We have known there must be other bears out there. We have searched for over a thousand years, since the days of Hegel. We had never found any though. Until I got lost, the bears of my village had never found a way to travel this far south."

"Yes … um … I got lost," Breckin said with an

embarrassed, Cub-like grin. "It was close to dusk and my group was searching for something for dinner, and I lost my way among the trees. I guess we all ended up searching for each other in all the wrong directions. I searched for them for over a week, traveling farther and farther south, since that was where we were supposed to be going. I came to the Barrier River, the farthest south bears from our village have ever come. It's a part of the Great River, cutting all the way through to the Salington Sea. I thought I would travel east as far as I could to search for my group, but there was no sign of them at all."

"The nights were cold and I slept wherever I could find some shelter. One night it was sleeting, and I was huddled in a narrow cave by the river. And I saw it. A marking on the wall."

Breckin looked around at the listening bears, his eyes wide as he remembered.

"The mark of Hegel! And a message from Heflin!"

8
Decisions

There were gasps of surprise, and C.J. dropped to his knees next to Merridy and Growly. "From Heflin!" he gasped.

"Yes!" Breckin said excitedly. "I couldn't believe it. No one knew what became of Heflin when he was lost at the Great River. According to our history books, the bears of his day hoped that he was with Janika and the others. But …"

C.J. was almost bursting with questions, but he knew that Breckin had a tale he must tell.

"Oh, I can't wait to learn about your history!" C.J. said, "but for now we need to know about you."

Breckin nodded, pausing for another sip of tea before he went on.

"Heflin's message," Breckin said excitedly. "It was about a way to travel under the Barrier River, through caves and a few short tunnels he had made with others. And about another place, far to the south … a place where it might be possible to find bears."

"Heflin!" C.J. whispered in astonishment, caught up completely in the story he was hearing.

"I followed the instructions, right under the river, coming out in the woods through a cave on the other side. From there I traveled east, all the way to the Great River, and then south, like Heflin's message had said. I ate whatever I could find along the way, which wasn't very much. Um, do you have any more pancakes?" he asked, looking up at Gittel with a bashful grin.

With a fresh stack of pancakes and a very happy Gittel, Breckin continued his story.

"The weather was getting very cold, with some storms of sleet. I knew that soon I would have to turn back. I don't even have a tent! It was right about that time that I saw the island and then came to The Precipice! We learn about The Precipice, from the days of Hegel, in our history classes. But I couldn't believe it when I saw it. And right there on the edge of the cliff were the two large boulders and the limestone caverns, just like Heflin's message said.

"I came out on the island, and through my telescope, I saw something flying. Bigger than the biggest bird I have ever seen. And I thought it was carrying something. Something that looked like it might be … a bear!

"That was me!" Skye burst out suddenly. The mention of flying was always exciting to her. "Breckin, I was flying a glider. We make them and fly them. I have been flying out near the banks watching for fires across the river. Ember saw one before the summer, and I was flying there yesterday while Chippy and Annily had their lessons."

"*You* were flying?" he asked Skye in wonder. It looked like he wanted to ask more questions, but then suddenly he remembered he was telling a story.

"Well, I started a signal fire, and then another, and another. I thought that if *you* were in trouble maybe another bear might see the smoke and come to help you."

"You're a brave Cub," Farren said softly, stepping forward and giving Breckin a pat on the shoulder, "to travel all this way on your own, trying to help the bears of your village."

Breckin looked down at the ground, feeling a little embarrassed, but there were tears in the corners of his eyes too. It had been very cold and scary and lonely out on his own.

"When I found out I couldn't get across the river …" The Cub's voice was beginning to tremble. "There was another message from Heflin, in a cave under the island. It said, 'No way further, heading North.' I had felt like I was so close to finding help. To have to turn back there …" Breckin's voice trailed off into a sniffle, and he wiped away a stray tear with his grimy coat sleeve.

"Well, you have found help!" Farren said encouragingly, and there were voices of agreement from those gathered all around.

Breckin looked up at Farren gratefully, "Thank you, sir." he said, his voice a little croaky.

Farren turned and gazed at the sky above the Great River and Heflin's Reach. Dark clouds stretched out to the west as far as he could see.

"Breckin, why don't you go with Gittel and Ash to find some fresh clothes and perhaps a basin of warm water to clean up a little. Rescue Committee, and the engineers, we will meet right here." There was an urgency in his voice that Growly was feeling in the pit of his stomach too. "C.J.," Farren said more quietly, stepping closer to the Elder bear, "would you look at those clouds through one of the telescopes and tell me what you think? Merridy, would you let me know what you think too?"

Just then, Growly's mother, Edolie, came running up the hillside. She had stayed in Haven longer to help coordinate the team preparing food. When she saw the look on her husband's face though, she slowed to a walk, her face worried and questioning as she came closer.

"What is it Farren?" she asked. She looked out toward the river and smoldering signal fires.

"Mama. A Cub was found out there and rescued by the eagles!" Growly said. "His whole village is in great danger."

"Yes," Farren said seriously. He pointed toward C.J. and Merridy, who were hurrying back from the telescopes. It was then that Edolie noticed the dark clouds out across the river.

"The first of the westerlies?" she asked, but it was hardly even a question. All bears knew what those type of clouds would most certainly mean.

"How long do you think?" Farren asked, as C.J. and Merridy came closer. Merridy was first to answer. She had a love of the seasons and a library full of books. When it came to the weather, Merridy was almost always the one to ask.

"A day, perhaps two," she said confidently, "but not much more than that. It is coming in slowly, but it is a westerly for sure. They will already be getting a good bit of snow over there, and we will be getting it soon too."

It was then that Chippy stepped forward. He had been watching all that had been happening, as Breckin was rescued and as he told his amazing story. And as Chippy listened an idea had been slowly forming, getting clearer and clearer as it grew and grew. When Breckin had left with Ash and Gittel, Chippy had run off to find paper and a pencil, calling Annily to follow so she could help him to think.

Now, as C.J. and Merridy talked earnestly with Farren, Chippy squeezed through the gathered bears, taking Growly's paw and leading him away.

"What is it?" Growly asked. "Bad weather is coming, Chippy. Do you have any ideas?"

It was Annily who spoke though. "Yes, Growly." She took a deep breath. "Show him, Chippy. Show him the paper that you drew."

When Growly came back up the hill just a short

time later, the whole hilltop was a hive of activity. Food supplies were being sorted and rationed; ropes, boards, and building materials were being counted. The engineering leaders were gathered, deep in discussion, and the Rescue Committee was sorting out hiking gear and packs.

Farren was still with C.J., Merridy, and Edolie, looking out across the river to the cloudy skies out in the west. Merridy was pointing to a particular formation, explaining its shape and color and all that could be told by looking at those things.

"It's hard to tell for sure," she was saying. "We probably won't experience it here for a little while yet, but over there it could be steady snows for weeks."

Growly, Chippy, and Annily walked up to the group slowly, Chippy with the papers in his trembling hand.

"Dad," Growly said softly, "Chippy has something which I think that you should see."

9

A Plan for a Rescue

Farren looked at the papers again, and then down at Chippy and Annily, as if he wanted to be sure they understood what was written there.

"You think this can work?" he asked quietly, and this time he knelt down on one knee so he could look directly into their eyes. "This is very dangerous. You do know that? Do you think that this can work?"

Chippy said nothing for a moment, but when he did, there was a sureness in his voice that made Farren blink. Sometimes it was easy to forget that Chippy was a very gifted inventor.

"It can work," he said, his accent adding a hint of adventure to the seriousness. "It *will* work."

"Dad," Growly said, "you see the weather that is coming in the west. This will be a very cold winter for the bears of Breckin's village. We must move quickly while there is still a chance. We are ready, if you believe this is the best thing to do.

Farren stood up and looked out toward the west

again, rubbing his ear nervously for a moment before he went back over to where C.J., Merridy, and Edolie were standing.

"How do you feel, Growly?" Chippy asked.

Growly smiled at his friend. The monkeys voice was kind and hopeful, and his accent always made Growly smile.

"It's scary, Chippy," Growly whispered, looking out toward the Great River.

"Scary like big waves on the Ocean?" Chippy said.

Growly nodded. "Just like that."

At that moment, Farren and Edolie walked over, followed closely by C.J and Merridy. As Growly's mother came closer, she reached down and hugged both Growly and the two monkeys, "It's a good plan Chippy, though it certainly makes me afraid. Farren is right though, we must help Breckin, and if we are going to help the bears of his village, we must move quickly."

"I'm going to go find Ember," C.J. added, "to see if we can talk more with the eagles. Merridy and your mother will gather extra supplies."

Farren put his hand on Growly's shoulder again and nodded to Chippy and Annily with a tired smile. "It *is* a good plan. A plan we must act on, I believe. Try and get a little rest now though. I will organize all that needs to be done."

With that, Farren strode off toward the engineers, calling the Rescue Committee to join him as he went.

Growly was just about to go and find some food

when Ember came running across the hilltop. As she reached Growly, she threw her arms around his neck, almost knocking him over. "Growly! I just heard. C.J. told me some …" Ember was trying not to cry, while also trying to catch her breath. She stepped back for a moment, looking at Growly as if she might never see him again. "I … it just felt like everything might be getting back to the way it was again." She looked at Annily then, and suddenly she stopped. "I'm sorry," she whispered, tears now flowing down her cheeks. "It's *not* the way it was anymore. Oh Annily, especially not for you." She threw her arms around her friend, hugging the young monkey tightly. "How can I say goodbye?"

Annily stood back for a minute, looking up at her friend with a grin. "You mean you didn't read the papers?"

Ember shook her head. "No, C.J. just told …"

"Oh Ember!" Annily cried happily. "You're coming too! That is, if … if you choose to." She added the last part seriously, looking down at her feet.

Ember looked at her three friends for a moment.

"Of course I will come, Annily," she said softly, putting her paw under her friends chin so she could see the monkey's eyes. "If it's a Chippy plan, I know it must be good."

Annily threw her arms around Ember, nodding in agreement.

"Now," Ember added, "where is it that I'm going to come?"

"It is a simple plan. It has to be," Farren said, speaking loudly so that everyone could hear above the gentle wind. "The first snows are coming. You all can see the clouds across the river."

There were nods of agreement.

"The first thing we must do is to find the bears of Arborstone. When Breckin left, they had very little food and nowhere warm to shelter through the winter. Breckin must lead the way, of course, but he shouldn't travel alone. Chippy suggested that he and Growly go, and I believe it is a good idea. A monkey will be easier for the eagles to carry, and a Young Bear like Growly can help to lead through the snow.

"And now," Farren said, looking around the bears huddled on the hilltop. "You all know the second part of the plan. It will be dangerous and difficult. It is also possible, I believe, if we don't give up."

The gathering ended then, with bears hurrying off to their assigned groups or rushing to gather ropes and prepare supplies.

Growly watched it all happening around him, a little unsure of what he should do. Ember and C.J. were down near the eagles, drawing on large sheets of paper as Goldentail watched from a distance. The eagles had stayed close by ever since Breckin arrived, perhaps watching to see what the bears might be planning to do next.

Annily and Chippy were huddled with some of the master engineers, led by Ruslan, who was nodding his head in agreement as Chippy pointed to one of the drawings.

A lot of the bears had already left for Haven. There were many things that would be needed from the village, and supplies would have to be brought in from some of the caverns and tunnels farther up in the mountains. If the bears of Breckin's village were to be helped, it would take a lot of work—work which had to begin right away.

"It's so hard to believe it is less than six months since you were a Cub, since we were standing in the hidden meadow that morning before your Adventure. Now look at you, Growly. Look at us. Who could believe that so much could change in so little time."

Growly looked up, startled from his thoughts by the voice of his mother. She was standing next to him now, watching the rush of activity all around.

"Yes, Mama," Growly said quietly. Since he had arrived back in Haven, nothing had felt the same. Perhaps it was the newness of being a Young Bear, he had thought over the weeks. And life had been so busy. He had been thinking that maybe once things settled down a little …

"It's never going to be the same again, is it?" he asked. "I guess, all the time I was gone, I wanted so badly to come back to Haven and get back to all that I had left behind. To drink tea and sing the old songs and maybe even write a book or two."

Edolie looked down at Growly and smiled. A gentle smile which had a little sadness in it.

"No Growly. It will *never* be the same." She put her arm around Growly's shoulder, giving him a hug. "But that doesn't mean that it can't be even better. Look. C.J. is home! You've seen the happy glow on Merridy's face. And monkeys! I've already heard at least fifteen songs about monkeys. The Cubs are singing them all day long. And they're playing that they're Adventurers!" she added with a laugh. "*Just like C.J. and Growly!*"

Growly grinned. He had seen the Cubs' Adventure games, and *their* Growlys acted a lot braver than he had ever felt.

"And now," Edolie continued, nodding toward the Great River, "the whole village is about to experience the greatest challenge we have ever known. Nothing will ever be the same after this."

Growly's mother was quiet for a long moment as she looked off into the distance. When she looked back at Growly though, there was a sparkle of hope and adventure in her eyes.

"We will still have our traditions though, and they can be even more meaningful than they were before. And our songs can be even more special … and a lot more silly too," she added with a grin.

"And we can still have our special foods," Growly laughed. "And *more*. Have you tried Annily's blackberry sweet bread?"

"Yes, Growly," Edolie said. The look on her face now though was serious and thoughtful. "Everything is about to change. But this first part … I'm so worried for you and Chippy, and for Annily and Ember. Please be careful, Growly." She turned and put a paw on each of his shoulders, looking at him lovingly as she said, "You will have a lot of books to write one day. I know a lot of Cubs who already want to read them."

She gave Growly another squeeze, pointing across the hillside to a figure who was hurrying in their direction. "I think it's almost time for you to leave," she said with a smile. "I'm sure you need to speak for a moment with part of your team."

Away

E mber was already dressed in her winter coat and pants, with heavy snow boots and a warm flight cap that went down over her ears. As she came across the hillside, Growly grinned and gave her a wave.

"I almost thought you were Skye for a moment," he laughed. "Well, at least your hat anyway." Growly looked down at his feet, and his voice was more serious when he continued. "Are you ready for this Ember? I mean … eagles!"

Ember smiled kindly, turning toward the Great River for a moment before she spoke. "Growly, I am *so* scared. And having some time to think about it makes it worse. The eagles will help us though. Look. Even more are coming in from the mountains. The ropes and harnesses are almost done. I think we will be leaving soon."

Growly nodded, trying to give Ember his bravest smile. "I guess I should get my coat and cap. I hope the eagles don't decide to go fishing!"

Ember let out a happy laugh, and it felt good to Growly to hear the sound of it in the midst of the wind and shouts and calls on the hilltop.

"It might not hurt for you to have a dip in the river before you get going to find Arborstone," Ember called happily. "Put a bar of soap in your coat pocket, Growly!"

Growly grinned as he stooped down to pick up his backpack, which had been filled with supplies for the coming journey.

"Don't forget your sleeping bag," Ash said. He had been working with the engineers, but now he came up beside Growly to help carry the pack over to where the ropes and harnesses lay stretched out on the grass. The afternoon sun was trying to peek through the thickening clouds, but it didn't bring much warmth from the icy breeze blowing up from the river.

"I hope you packed an extra pair of socks," he added, patting Growly affectionately on the back.

Growly nodded and shivered. "I know. It's already getting cold."

Ash's face lit up with a wide grin. "Well, I was meaning to make sock puppets. It's always good to have some of those."

It was Growly's turn to laugh this time. A loud, long, happy laugh that startled everyone around.

Ash had always made him laugh like that, ever since they had been Little Cubs. It wasn't even so much what he said that was so funny, but the way he said it. Sometimes he might just say something like, "I believe I finally understand what Hitherhall meant," and then just stop, with such a contented, knowing look on his face that you almost believed that there once was a bear named Hitherhall, and that Ash finally did understand whatever it was Hitherhall might have said. And then would come that wide, carefree grin and a look in his eyes that led to howls of laughter.

It felt good to hear laughter on the hilltop. Everyone had been rushing with their assigned tasks. Important tasks. But there had been a growing feeling of worry that everyone could sense. No bear from Haven had ever crossed the Great River. Not since the days of Hegel. And there hadn't been a river there then.

There were many risks. The winds above the river were too dangerous for gliders. The eagles would do their best; Ember was sure of that. But still, the weather was getting worse and anything could happen.

And then there was the second part of Chippy's plan. The part that would require all the bears of Haven. There were many dangers in that too, and much that could go wrong.

Farren looked up at the sound of Growly's laugh, and his face lightened a little from the tiredness and worry that had been there.

"The mayor shouldn't be working on harnesses," Growly said with a smile. "And where is your coat and top hat?"

Farren got to his feet, laying the harness he was checking back on the ground.

"I've checked them three times so far," he said. "It's good to hear your laugh though, Growly. There is so much to be done and so much that can go wrong. I'm not sure I'm ready for times like these."

"Well, times like these need a laugh sometimes, I think," said Growly. "Chippy taught me that when I was feeling like you do now."

Farren glanced over at the monkey, who was deep in conversation with C.J., Annily, and Ruslan. Chippy was dressed in a winter coat with the hood pulled up over his head, thick winter pants, and warm snow boots. He had been dressing this way for weeks now. It never got very cold in his home of Towerwood, and he was not used to this weather at all.

"I'm glad Chippy is going with you," Farren said softly, putting his paw on Growly's shoulder. "He would be of great help here. His ideas are ingenious, but I just have a feeling you are going to need him, Growly, perhaps to see a way where you can't see one on your own. Friends can help in that way sometimes, and he is the truest of friends."

Farren took a long, deep breath. "Now, I think you should go and say your goodbyes quickly. It is time for you to leave."

Goldentail circled above the hilltop, letting out loud calls to the other eagles. Some flew off in twos with the bears' (and monkey's) backpacks clasped tightly between them. Others were lining up along the stretched out ropes, testing their grip on the knots that would help them as they carried the weight of Growly and his companions.

Chippy and Breckin would be the easiest. Breckin was a good deal smaller than Growly, and Chippy was smaller than them both. So the largest of the eagles were gathered along Growly's ropes, and Goldentail would take their lead.

Growly stood on the hillside with his harness strapped tight around his waist and shoulders. His heart was thumping hard as he looked out toward the Great River, feeling the icy, stinging wind whipping up from the west. They would have to hurry if they were to do all that was needed to be done before the snow.

"Woo-hoo!"

Growly was shaken from his thoughts by Chippy's shout. It was always hard to tell with Chippy if that sound was joy or panic. After all their travels, Growly was pretty sure it was a little bit of both.

The monkey was running down the side of the hill, with the eagles stretching up into the air in front of him, gripping the ropes tightly in their talons. All of a sudden, there was a mighty tug, and Chippy leapt into the air, howling with a sound that was much *less* joy and a lot *more* panic.

Breckin was right behind him, racing down the

hillside and then whooshing up into the air as the
eagles strained up into the wind.

"Now Growly!" C.J. called. He had a small flag in
his paw, which he waved in case Growly hadn't heard.

Growly took off at a run, picking up speed as he
raced down the hillside, doing his best not to stumble
before the eagles could lift him off the ground. All of a
sudden he felt a powerful tug on the ropes, and with
all his might he leapt up into the air, feeling the
strength of the eagles wings suddenly lift him high up
above the slope of the hillside. The wind howled
around his ears, mixed with the calls of the eagles and
the distant, muffled sound of Chippy's howls.

Chippy was already at the edge of the Great River,
and as the eagles carrying him strained upward and
out over the roaring water, Growly was terrified to see
the young monkey swerve and sway and twist in the
buffeting wind. Breckin was right behind him, swaying
and rocking as he clung to his harness. There wasn't
time to think about it though. In a moment, Growly
reached the river's edge and felt the jolting bast of the
wind. A muffled cry from Goldentail sounded like it
was coming from somewhere far, far away. All Growly
could do was to cling desperately to the ropes, while he
dangled and swung over the rushing torrent.

Icy spray and sleet were in the air, and they pelted
against Growly's face, stinging his eyes and cheeks,
even through his thick fur. It was hard to see anything
at all, and his paws ached, as if he had been holding
on to the ropes for hours. All of a sudden, he saw a

huge, blurry form up ahead of him, and he took a shaky paw off the ropes for a second to wipe his eyes as the shape of Heflin's Reach towered up and into view.

Growly gasped. The eagles were swinging around on a strong downdraft, doing their best to keep him steady as they came swooping down through the trees. Growly felt branches and bristles all around him, swinging and swaying on the ropes as the eagles flew through the forest. Goldentail's voice could be heard above all the noise around, calling loudly as they swung through the last of the pines, and then, suddenly, Growly felt solid ground and soft grass as he tumbled to his knees.

11
ʟandings

Chippy was already out of his harness, and in a moment he was at Growly's side with Breckin following close behind. The two of them helped unfasten the straps, coiling the ropes quickly so that the eagles could more easily carry them back across the river. It wasn't long until the three companions were standing next to their backpacks, watching the eagles soar out over the water, back toward the bears on the hill on the other side.

Growly's heart was still pounding, and he could see that Breckin was panting heavily and Chippy looked very shaky on his feet. Growly lifted his trembling, aching paws to his face, breathing on them to try and warm them up.

"That was ..." He felt his whole body tremble. "Wow." It was not the exciting kind of wow.

Chippy just nodded. His teeth were chattering with the cold, but in a few moments the frightened look started to melt, and his face lit up with a warm smile.

"Eagles, Growly! We flew with eagles!"

Growly grinned. "I … I think I'm more a *glider* kind of bear!"

Breckin let out a laugh now too. He had been on the edge of tears after a rough landing.

"Come on, " Chippy said suddenly. "We will need to hurry to be ready for the next part." He stooped down and took hold of the long ropes attached to Breckin's harness. Breckin untied the last of the straps, taking the harness completely off and winding the ropes into two coils, one of which Chippy flung over his shoulder before taking off at a run towards the trees.

Growly fumbled with his cold, aching paws to untie a small saw, which had been attached to his backpack. Finally he got the ties free, and with Breckin by his side, ran to the grove of trees on the north end of the island. Chippy was already there, scrambling up into the branches of a tall, majestic pine that towered above the others.

"Here!" he called, pointing to a place on the trunk of the tree high above. "We'll cut this branch."

Growly could barely see Chippy through the jumble of pine needles and twigs, but he nodded and handed the saw to Breckin.

"Are you ok to climb?" Growly asked seriously.

Breckin's eyes were wide and he was still trembling from the flight across the river, but an excited smile spread across his face.

"Growly, I love climbing," the Cub said proudly. Tying the saw handle quickly to his belt, he swung up into the branches.

With Breckin on his way, Growly ran back to where the eagles had placed their packs along with other supplies. There was a large, rolled up tent, as well as another roll of rope netting. A bag lay beside it filled with tools. At the bottom of the bag, Growly found a pouch filled with large metal spikes, the kind the bears of Haven used when making tree houses and lookouts in the forest. Taking the bag and the rolled up net, Growly hurried back to the tree where Chippy and Breckin were already busy sawing. There were twigs and leaves strewn about at the foot of the tree, and as Growly came closer, he was almost knocked over by a large branch that came crashing down from above.

"I ... I'm down here!" Growly called, his heart thumping from the near miss.

"Sorry, Growly!"

Chippy's voice could be heard from somewhere up above, and then his face appeared through the branches as he peered down at Growly through the leaves.

There was another sound of something coming through the leaves, and then a thump as that something hit Growly on the head.

"Ropes coming!" came a shout from above. It was Breckin, and he sounded very proud to be helping.

Growly grinned up at Chippy. The rope on his head hadn't hurt—well, too much.

Growly quickly tied the tool bag and netting to the rope, as Chippy disappeared back up into the branches to help Breckin haul it up. While the rope lifted upward, Growly noticed the afternoon was getting darker and darker as the clouds continued to gather from the west. There wouldn't be snow tonight. All bears could tell when it was about to snow. It would be very cold though, and Growly had a lot to do to prepare.

Leaving the tree, he ran back to the pile of packs and supplies. In one of the pockets he found the small telescope he had packed, and in a moment he was scrambling up onto one of the large boulders in the clearing. From up there, he could see farther to the north and a long way back down the island to the south. With the telescope up to his eye, he looked all around the clearing, taking note of the boulders and caves and grassy places where it would be best to set up camp. It had to be sheltered from the wind, as much as possible, and a good cave nearby would be helpful in case of emergency. It should be visible from the hill on the other side of the river. There!

Growly slid down the edge of the boulder and onto the grass, running as fast as he could back to the supplies. With the rolled up tent over his shoulder, he took off again, running a short distance to the south, where there was a grassy nook surrounded by boulders

and rocks. There was plenty of room for the tent, and
before too long Growly had it securely in place, with a
wide piece of canvas stretched out over a nearby cave
as well.

"They're coming! Growly, they're coming!"

It was Breckin. The Cub was running across the
clearing and pointing out over the Great River at two
small shapes swinging high above the water, carried
along by the power of the straining eagles. Growly
could hear the distant calls and cries now, muffled but
sure amongst all the noise of the wind and the river.
The two shapes were swinging wildly in the wind. The
weather had gotten much worse than when he had
come across earlier. The smaller of the two shapes
suddenly veered to the left, pushed along northward
on a strong gust.

Chippy was running out into the clearing now too,
waving his arms frantically.

The other shape was in deep trouble too, swinging wildly to the left and then suddenly dropping for a moment, before an enormous gust lifted the figure again and thrust it forward toward the island. The same powerful rush of wind knocked Growly over, sending him tumbling to the ground as the dangling figure went whooshing overhead.

"Ember!" Growly cried. For a moment he saw her frightened face as she hurtled by, swinging wildly as the eagles tried to get control against the wind. Goldentail swooped past, pulling his wings in tight as he shot upward. Growly could hear him crying out to the other eagles.

In a moment Growly was back on his feet, racing after Ember as she twisted on the ropes. She was swinging too wildly for the eagles to let her go. There were rocks and boulders everywhere, and the howling gale was quickly pushing her out toward the other side of the island. Other eagles were swooping in now, circling in and trying to help as Ember was blown along.

Growly could hear his heart pounding in his ears, and he gasped for breath as he raced under the dangling ropes. They were almost at the far edge of the island now. He bounded up the side of a large boulder, his boots slipping a little as he fumbled in his coat pocket for his pocket knife. There.

"Growly!" Ember's frightened cry was just behind him. The eagles were fighting against the wind as best they could, but they were still being blown out of control. Growly leaped out into the air, barely catching one of the ropes. Clinging with one paw, Growly sawed desperately at the rope with his knife. They were still being blown, and they were almost out of time.

The eagles were trying to fly lower, but the powerful wind was driving them upward. All of a sudden, the knife cut through the rope, loosening Ember's harness and letting them both drop lower on the other rope. "There!" Growly cried, seeing a wide stretch of grass near the edge of the island.

Goldentail saw it too. The mighty eagle let out an echoing cry to the eagles carrying the other rope. Suddenly, Growly and Ember were falling, and then, with a jolting thud, tumbling through the long, tangling grass.

Growly lay still for a moment, his head spinning and heart pounding, before he leaped to his feet again. "Ember!"

Ember was slowly climbing to her feet, wobbling and unsteady as she fumbled with her harness. Taking a deep breath, a shaky smile started to form at the corners of her mouth, and she was just about to say something when a cry came from somewhere far away.

"Annily!" Growly recognized Breckin's voice, somewhere up near the woods where they had been working. Then there was a second cry, and this one filled Growly with alarm.

"Annily!" It was Chippy and his voice was panicked and afraid.

12
Underneath the River

As Growly came racing around one of the largest boulders in the clearing, he saw Breckin waving frantically at the edge of the trees. Chippy's voice could be heard somewhere off behind him, calling out in alarm.

"Annily!" There was no sound of her reply, just the roar of the water and the wind and the cries of eagles.

"They were blown off course," Breckin gasped as Growly and Ember finally reached him. "Chippy and I were watching from the boulders when she was caught by a gust and blown up river. We lost sight of her behind the trees, and now…"

"Come on," Growly said. "We need to help Chippy search the woods, and it will take all of us."

Breckin sniffed and nodded bravely.

Suddenly, there was a rush of movement from the trees—eagles swerving and turning past the boughs and branches and bursting out into the clearing. As they saw the bears, they swooped down low, circling around them with cries of alarm. Then they were off again, into the trees in the same direction from which they had come.

"That way!" Ember shouted. "They want us to follow!"

In a moment, she was off at a run, dashing amongst the towering pines with Growly and Breckin right behind. They could hear the calls of the eagles somewhere up ahead, a shrill, urgent sound that made the bears run even faster as they leapt over broken branches and kicked up fallen leaves.

As Growly raced along, he saw Chippy a little way ahead. The monkey disappeared for a moment under some tall ferns and then burst out again on the other side.

"Chippy!" Growly called. "The eagles are over at that tree!"

Chippy skidded to a halt for a moment, startled by Growly's voice. When he saw where Growly was pointing though, he nodded and took off again, racing toward a tall pine with low, stretching branches and a thick covering of leaves. There were eagles standing in front of it, and calls from others higher in the tree. Chippy didn't even stop as he came close. With a sudden leap he sprung up onto a low bough and then disappeared up into the heights.

There was no sound for a moment, and then suddenly, Chippy's voice.

"Annily!" This time it was a cry of joy, filled with sudden relief.

She had been blown up river, as the eagles

carrying her struggled to turn against the sudden blast of wind. Another crosswind had caught them then, sending them speeding suddenly back toward the island and into the trees. Annily was laughing now as she told the story, though it had taken her a while to stop shaking after they got her down from the tree.

She had been attached to a thin, strong line, which Breckin had untangled from the branches of the tree. The line had been prepared up on the hill across the river earlier, tied together from long spools which had been carried from the Westwind Caverns.

One end of the line had been tied to Annily's harness, and as the eagles flew out over the raging river, the lightweight line had stretched out behind her, wound out safely by Ruslan and the engineers on the hill. On and on it had stretched, the longest length of line any bear had known of in the history of Haven. Spool after spool until finally, Annily reached the island ... and the trees!

It was an important part of the plan, and for the last hour the five of them had been working to get it in place. Growly and the others had tied their end high in the branches of the tree that Chippy and Breckin had been working on, and the bears on the hill across the river had tied their end to a strong tower, which was now being built on the hilltop.

Chippy had set up wheels and a pulley on a platform he and Breckin had started in the branches. Tomorrow the thin line would be tied to a thick, very strong length of rope which would be pulled above the river and tied to the pulley.

"Zip line," Chippy said with a grin, pointing toward the plans. "More bears here to help. More supplies. Then cables. Strong cables and strong towers. It can be done." He said it with a nod, as if to assure himself.

Annily put her arm around his shoulder and hugged him tightly. "It will be," she said confidently. "It's a good plan Chippy, and we will get it done. I think almost every bear in Haven is working on it now. Probably even the Baby Cubs!" She laughed for a moment, but then her eyes suddenly filled with tears. "Oh, be safe, Chippy!"

The entrance to the cave was toward the south end of the island, a small opening amongst the boulders in the middle of another thicket of trees. As they disappeared into the darkness, Growly took one last look at the two figures standing back out in the dim afternoon light.

Annily had her head down, and even from this distance he could hear her gentle sobs, and Ember's comforting voice. Annily and Chippy would have been married by now if they hadn't come to help him climb The Precipice. They had been cut off from their home and the friends and family they loved. And now Chippy was going out on a dangerous journey. Annily had always been a brave monkey, but even the bravest ones cry at times. That's a part of being brave.

Ember was there with her arm around Annily's shoulder, peering down into the darkness of the tunnel. Since Growly had come home to Haven with C.J., he and Ember had spent time talking about all that had happened and about what might lie ahead.

He was a Young Bear now, no longer a Cub. She would be a librarian, working with Merridy and C.J. on language books and maps, as well as cataloging all that had been learned in C.J.'s travels. Growly was going to write a book or two as well, as soon as he could help Chippy and Annily get home. And then … Growly looked up at Ember one last time. And then I can finally be at home, with everything right and in its right place.

"It's just down here."

Breckin's voice startled Growly out of his thoughts. They had come around a bend and now stood in a large cavern. Breckin held his lantern up higher, pointing to a place on the far wall. Growly hurried over and stood next to Chippy, who was gazing up at the ancient words in wonder.

"What does it say, Growly? It looks like Bear. Is it?"

Growly nodded. It *was* bear. Old Bear. He had learned some of it as a Cub. All of Hegel's writings were translated from Old Bear, and some of the best songs still had a line or two in that ancient language. It made a song seem more important, even if you didn't know what you were singing. And some of the words sounded very funny, like your tongue was wobbly and tangled.

Growly looked up at the writings, doing his best to make out the words.

"It's a poem, I think," Growly whispered. "This line says '*To the westward winds and westwoods blown. To Northgate and the bridge to home.*' There's some more here that I can't make out, and ..." Growly gasped. "Janika! It says something about Janika that I can't make out. And there is *Heflin*! Signed right at the bottom! It's the message you saw, Breckin. '*No way further. Heading North.*' " Growly's heart was pounding. "This is incredible! C.J. and Merridy could read it. They could read it all. It's a message from Heflin! From a thousand years ago!"

Chippy whistled, shaking his head in wonder.

"There are more writings like that in the other tunnel too, at the Barrier River." Breckin said. "A lot more."

"Oh, I wish I could stay here and study these!" Growly said with a groan. "Or at least write them down. We have to keep moving though. We might have one more day before the snowstorm hits. Once that happens, things are going to get very difficult. We're going to have to push hard, through the night and all day tomorrow if we can. Are you ready?"

Breckin nodded seriously, and Chippy gave Growly a determined grin. "Like old times, Growly, but colder."

Growly laughed then. "Yes Chippy! A *lot* colder."

With lanterns held high, they took off at a jog deeper into the tunnel. At places, there were deep caverns with stalactites and stalagmites, and in others, gurgling streams bubbling out of dark crevices and hidden places. And all the while they heard the deep, trembling rumble of the Great River somewhere up above.

In some places, the tunnel was so narrow Growly had to take off his backpack and turn sideways to squeeze through, with Chippy and Breckin helping till they got past the narrow place. On and on they went, crouching under low places and leaping over deep pools until finally Growly felt the wonderful, familiar feeling of fresh air on his face, and they stepped out into a sight no bear of Haven, at least in a thousand years, had ever seen before.

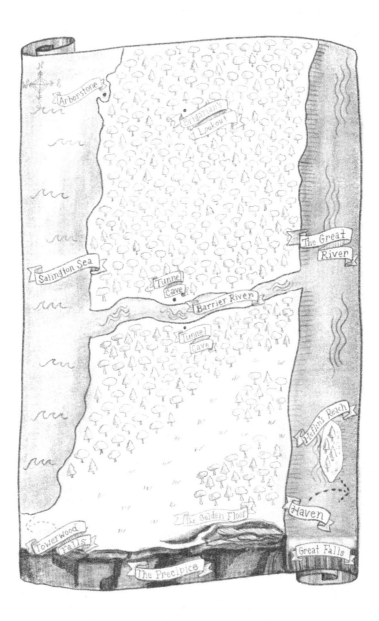

13

Beyond the Golden Floor

I n the oldest of the history books, *The Tales of Hegel and the Bears of Whistiglen*, there is a place described near the edge of The Precipice. It is mentioned in the chapter before the great tragedy as the last place the bears of the Southern Search made their camp together.

> *"Our tents were pitched in amongst the trees, looking out over the astonishing sight that stretched out along The Precipice. All was stone, as far as the eye could see—flat stone, with streaks and swirls of orange, red, and yellow, like a painting that stretched on for miles, bursting with color in the late afternoon light. It filled our hearts with hope, and the Little Cubs danced around in happy circles, singing out the old, silly songs. We all did."*

As they came out between the two large boulders at the end of the tunnel, Growly felt his heart leap in astonishment. *The Golden Floor!* One of the Little Cubs in Hegel's time had called it that, and that is the name

that had stayed. Growly had hardly dared to believe
there could be such a place. He had thought perhaps it
was a legend that had grown with time. But, seeing it
now …

Chippy gasped and blinked a few times to make
sure he was really seeing what stretched out in front of
him. The sun was almost setting in the west, and its
light flooded the stone with color, almost a reflection
of the stunning sunset piercing through the clouds.

Growly sighed. How he would love to sit out here
on the *The Golden Floor* with Chippy and Breckin,
eating apples around an open fire like the bears of
Hegel's day. They had to keep moving though. Those
clouds looked beautiful now, but they carried snow.

With their lanterns lit, they took off at a quick
pace, moving into the forest that stretched along the
edge of the Great River. There would be long, open
meadows farther to the north. This would make
traveling a lot faster, at least until the snow arrived. If
they had good weather through the night and through
the day tomorrow, there was a chance they might be
able to reach the Barrier River (which Breckin had
mentioned), by nightfall.

Traveling in the woods at night was not easy.
There were roots and hidden holes and slippery
places, and it was always hard to make sure you were
going in the right direction.

"Keep the roar of the river closely on your right,"
C.J. had told them, and it was very good advice.
Almost as good as Merridy's.

"Make sure to stop and eat some chocolate from time to time, with the roar of the river closely on your right, of course!" she added with a grin.

As the night wore on, they made good distance, moving up along the edge of the Great River with their lanterns swinging as they ran. At midnight they stopped for dinner: sandwiches and dried fruit with a piece of chocolate for dessert. And then, just before the sunrise, they rested for a short while under the trees.

When morning light began to glow to the east, they were running again through the open fields, which stretched out over the miles as they journeyed northward along the banks of the Great River. Flurries of snow swirled in the air, and the winds that blew up from the river were icy and biting.

As the day wore on they came to forests again, tall evergreens with thick stretches of fern. When the way got too difficult, they cut as close as they safely could to the water, running along the bank of the Great River so they could move more quickly. They couldn't stay there long. The weather was getting worse by the hour, and the winds kicked up icy spray, which clung to their clothes and fur.

"There!" Breckin gasped, pointing with one paw as he took a moment to catch his breath. They were at the top of a small hill, looking down over another forest to a faint glimmer amongst the trees. "You can't see it from here. We're too low. But it's the Barrier River, and it's very wide."

Growly looked up at the darkening sky, his face a mixture of relief and concern. It would be dark in less than an hour, and the full storm was brewing overhead. Growly looked carefully at Chippy and Breckin. They both looked as exhausted as he felt. It seemed like every muscle in his body was aching, and he desperately wanted to lie down and get some sleep.

"Do you think you can go farther?" he asked quietly, but he already knew what their answer would be. It was a joke they had been sharing as they had raced along through the day.

"As long as we have chocolate!" they all said at once. Though this time it seemed that they *hoped* it was true.

"Breckin, how far to the east till we reach the tunnel? Do you think you can remember?"

Breckin grinned. "I got lost for a few hours last time, following a bee. When I got back to the river … maybe five hours?"

Growly felt his heart sink. He was so tired. The tunnel would be their best chance of shelter in a blizzard though. "That's a lot better than six," he said with a tired smile.

"A bed and then breakfast," Chippy sighed. "Well, a sleeping bag and a piece of chocolate. Come on Growly, let's go.

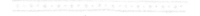

As they reached the trees, the snow was getting stronger, with thick, heavy flakes that whipped up against them as they pushed into the forest. It was better under the branches, but the biting wind still howled around them, and when Growly looked up, he could already see a light covering on the branches in the last of the sunlight up above.

Reaching the Barrier River, they turned quickly westward, racing amongst the boulders and over the fallen logs along the open stretch of the riverbank. The river was wide. Growly could see the other side far, far in the distance. In between, all was rushing water and roaring rapids, just like the Great River.

As darkness fell, they lit their lanterns, moving in amongst the trees as the snow got heavier. It was already thick on the ground along the edge of the river and was forming drifts along the sides of the boulders.

On they pushed. They were all gasping as they ran now. It was hard to breathe in the icy wind, and they were desperately tired. They did stop once, for chocolate, of course, and to rest for a moment in a small cave, but then they were off again along the river.

It was past midnight when they saw it, a thick, long pine tree, fallen and caught between three large boulders. "It's just past here!" cried Breckin. "Just back in the woods. There are more boulders, a whole lot of them, and in amongst them is the cave.

"Are you sure this is it?" Growly asked. It was very hard to see now in the driving wind and snow.

Breckin nodded excitedly. He was covered in snow, with just small tufts of fur visible around his face and eyes. They all looked like that, with hoods pulled up tight, and icicles clinging to their fur. Chippy was almost lost in his heavy coat, but his grin was as wide and warm as ever, even if his teeth were chattering in the cold.

"Show us the way, Breckin," Growly said, and the Cub took off at a run into the woods, with Growly and Chippy close behind. They pushed through a deep stretch of fern and up a steep bank till they saw the dark shadows of the boulders in amongst the trees.

Breckin disappeared into a narrow space between two of the larger rocks, sticking his head back out a few moments later to wave them on.

"We're here!" he beamed, leading them through into a small cave opening and then down into a tunnel. "It's much shorter than the other one, and there is a bigger cave on the other side."

The tunnel was like the one under the Great River, some larger natural caverns joined by narrow tunnels and smaller caves. There were a few places where Growly could see the ancient marks of chisels and digging, the work of Heflin and his friends so long ago. Like before, the river rumbled above them. It made all of them feel uneasy, and when they finally began climbing upward and the rumbling fell behind them, they began to joke and talk about how good it would be to sleep.

"I could sleep on a pile of pinecones," Growly said with an exhausted laugh.

"My pinecones don't even need to be piled," Breckin chuckled, putting his arm tiredly over Chippy's shoulder.

The cave on the other side of the river was a lot bigger, with a level floor and a good place in the middle for an open fire. There was plenty of wood around, some of it even dry, and soon they had a blazing fire going and ate a meal of freshly roasted potatoes and hot tea.

Chippy was already sleeping now, wrapped up in his sleeping bag with just his eyes and nose showing through the tightly bundled hood. Breckin did his best to keep his eyes open—his eyelids sinking lower and lower until finally he fell blissfully into sleep.

Growly looked out into the darkness for a moment. The wind was howling past the entrance of the cave, pushing heavy swirls of snow in amongst the trees. Tomorrow was going to be a very difficult day. But tonight … with a yawn, he stretched out on the floor, and fell instantly to sleep.

14

Blizzard

Chippy awoke to the sound of howling wind and the chattering of his teeth in the bitter cold. The fire had gone out sometime in the night, and drifts of snow were already building up at the entrance of the cave.

Snow would be more wonderful, Chippy had decided, if it didn't come with all that cold. It was still wonderful though. Even now Chippy felt his heart beating excitedly as he looked out on the swirling rush of white. The flakes were thick and heavy in the wind, sailing past the cave front in a twisting, howling dance.

In Towerwood, it never snowed. Chippy felt a sudden, unexpected ache in his heart as he thought of his home. His mother and father and his little sister Eka. Meegwin and Aila, the librarians. And Tappen, Jacory, and Barbod, his friends since he was little. Oh how he missed them all!

His mother and father would be lighting the fire and serving hot drinks on a cold winter morning like this. That thought made Chippy smile. A cold winter day in Towerwood meant you probably shouldn't go swimming, and if you just happened to fall in the water, you should not stay there long, but head home and put on some dry clothes. Chippy had not even seen snow until he glimpsed it far away on the mountaintops of the Alps. Now it was all around him, and Towerwood felt very, very far away. They would find a way back down, he and Growly and the bears of Haven, but oh how he missed it right now.

As he lay on the cold floor of the cave, he thought about his family. How terrible it must have been when they found out he was missing, trapped above The Precipice and unable to come home.

Eka would have cried and cried. She was still so little. She loved to ride on Chippy's shoulders. He would carry her all around the village and she would cry out excitedly, "I'm as big as Remiki! I'm as big as Remiki!" Of course, no one knew how big the founder of Towerwood really was, but in Eka's eyes, Remiki was about as big as any monkey could possibly ever be.

Chippy wiped a tear out of his eyes as he sat up. Oh, how he missed his little sister.

"Growly … Breckin," he whispered, shaking his friend's foot, and reaching out to the Cub. "Deep snow."

Growly sat up with a jolt, looking around with bleary eyes in the dim light. Breckin snorted, slowly opening one eye and then the other, before he sat up and grinned at Chippy.

"Ch ... ch ... ch ... Chippy! C ... c ... can you h ... hear your t ... t ... t ... teeth ch ... ch ... chattering?"

When Breckin realized his teeth were chattering too, he grinned and put his paw up to his chin, as if to try and keep it closed. That got them all roaring with laughter, which felt very good in the icy dampness of the cave.

Growly looked out into the squall outside and at the tall drifts that were growing larger and larger at the entrance to the cave.

"There will be no time for a hot breakfast this morning," he said sadly. "The snow is getting higher quickly. Breckin, can you show me the map you brought from your village? If we can stick to the forests, I think we can still travel fairly quickly in this blizzard."

Breckin nodded, handing Growly a large, folded map from a pocket in his backpack.

"I wish we could wait out the storm," Growly said seriously, "but it could go on for a long time. Without much shelter, the bears of your village are in great danger. We will have to go as quickly as we can."

It was a breakfast of nuts and dried fruit, and that's what meals were going look like for a while, apart from the times they would be able to roast acorns and potatoes on a fire as they camped. As they finished up, Growly unstrapped the snowshoes he had fastened to his pack.

"We're going to need these for a while," he said, pointing to the map. "There's a small stretch of forest here, but beyond that are open hills. I think it will be well after midday when we get back into the trees."

With their snowshoes firmly on, they stepped out into the gale, taking long, steady steps as they pushed against the wind. They all had their flight goggles on, with hoods pulled tight and thick scarves wrapped all the way up above their noses. Before they left the trees, they each had found long sticks, which they held in each paw (and hand) as poles to help them walk.

Out over the open fields they slogged, making their way over the thick drifts of snow that shifted and slid under their snowshoes. The hills were slick and icy in places, with treacherous holes to watch out for. Many times someone fell, sliding downward until the others could help him up again. Before leaving the cave they had tied themselves together with rope, and when someone tripped or fell, it would jolt the others. They were thankful they were all tied together. It would be terrible, and easy, to be separated and lost in the blinding whiteness of the blizzard.

Finally, they came to the trees again, and there were moments of shelter from the howl of the wind. They all had icicles on their coats and under their noses, and as they stopped in the shelter of a small forest cave for a moment, Chippy pulled down his frozen scarf and grinned. He was covered in a crust of icy snow, with just the sparkle of his eyes showing behind his goggles, and a wide, chattering smile, spread across his face.

It was easier traveling in the forests. Though the ground was sometimes rough and uneven, the trees blocked some of the wind and snow, and there were many boulders and small caves where they could stop to eat and find shelter at night. Breckin led them steadily northward for many days, being sure to watch for landmarks or any signs that would show them where they might be on the map. It was hard to see much in the snow. The blizzard continued day and night, howling and whistling through the trees and covering everything in white.

They had been traveling almost five days when Breckin suddenly shouted in excitement, pointing through the pelting snow to a towering shape up ahead amongst the trees. "Brigarian's Lookout!" he exclaimed, trying to be heard above the wind. "I've been there before! I've been there before!"

It was a tall tower of rock, made of large boulders and weathered granite in the middle of the trees. It was not bear made, though a bear named Brigarian had discovered it long ago. Perhaps there had once been a mountain here that had worn away with wind and weather and rain and snow and time. Large boulders stood strewn amongst the trees, and more surrounded the tall spire of stone in the clearing. The spire was riddled with holes and caves, and small, scraggly trees grew high on its summit.

"This way!" Breckin shouted, leading them through the boulders and onward around the spire till they came to the other side. The Cub pulled down his scarf, and his proud, happy smile cracked through the snow and ice around his cheeks. "We'll sleep well tonight!" he exclaimed excitedly. "On beds!"

He pointed to a large, wooden door at the base of the spire, almost covered by a drift but still bright and red in the dimness of the blizzard. In a moment, they had their shovels out, digging through the snow until soon the door stood wide open and they were hurrying inside. With the door tightly shut again, they dropped their packs to the floor, and Breckin hurried across the wide cave to light a lantern in the corner. There were other lanterns hung as well, and window holes and air vents twisted up out of the room.

Growly looked around in wonder. It was a natural cave, the size of a small home, with different levels and stairs connecting through the room. There was a large, round glass window next to the door they had just entered, mostly covered by snow outside. There were eight beds in all: four on the lower floor, two on a raised area on the far side, and two more in a loft built up toward the roof of the cave. A couch and chairs were circled around a fireplace, which had a chimney going up and out of sight against the wall. There was also a simple kitchen with pots and pans and a stack of worn, wooden plates.

"Does somebody live here?" Chippy asked in wonder, loosening his jacket and laying his scarf over one of the seats.

Breckin shook his head. "Bears from my village come here to stay while foraging in the warmer months. There are fruit trees all around. Apples, pears, oranges—all kinds of things. We dry and preserve and bottle it and then take it all back home."

"So we are close!" Growly said excitedly. He had been wondering if perhaps they had gone disastrously off course in the storm.

Breckin nodded, his eyes bright. " Just two days in good weather." The Cub looked toward the snow covered window. "Maybe three," he added with a weary smile. "Now, who would like some stewed peaches?"

That evening they sat cozily around the fire, talking happily in the warmth of the cave as the blizzard roared outside. There was plenty to eat here, and they roasted potatoes and nuts on the open fire.

Breckin sang them songs from his village of Arborstone—songs about the Salington Sea and the ice drifts that floated by in the winter. He also told them about his life and family. He had three brothers and a younger sister, and his parents built the best canoes in all of the village. One day he was going to be an inventor, just like Chippy, and build a boat that could sail all the way across the Salington Sea.

As he listened, Growly felt a growing feeling of hope rising up inside him. Three days. Even in this blizzard they could make this last stretch easily. But as they sat there drinking hot tea, they had no idea of the danger just a little way ahead.

Ropes

The morning started well, with a hot breakfast and steaming mugs of tea around the fire before dawn. They would head west along a low ridge for a few miles, and then down into forests again, which would take them all the way to the Salington Sea. From there, Breckin assured them, it would be easy to find the flooded ruins of Arborstone, and the many hundreds of stranded bears who were camped out nearby.

As the faint glow of the sun gave a little light around them, the three companions pushed out into the blizzard again, their snowshoes crunching on the fresh drifts that had built up overnight.

Breckin was in the lead this morning. He knew this area well, though he had never been here in the winter. "We will be under the trees for another mile," he shouted, doing his best to be heard above the roar of the wind. "Then we will reach the ridge. I will let you know when we are getting close."

As they slogged on through the snow, Growly

thought back on all that Breckin had shared the night before. There were some funny stories about his brothers and sister, and about life in Arborstone, on the edge of the water.

But there was one thing he had told them that kept coming back to mind—a fire across the Barrier River. Back in the spring, a bear who had been out exploring thought he saw a fire across the water, near to the place where the two rivers meet. No one was sure what to think of it then, but when Arborstone was flooded, it was thought perhaps it could mean help.

When Growly heard about the fire, he felt his heart leap, and he remembered something Ember had told him back on Heflin's Reach.

"Growly," she had said, her face looking puzzled. "I saw fire across the Great River back in the spring. The day you left to go on your Adventure. If it wasn't made by Breckin, or someone from his village, then who? It wasn't from lightning, Growly. I have thought about it often, and I know that it wasn't."

Growly hadn't had an answer then. He had looked at her quietly and slowly shook his head.

"I think there might be others Growly. Maybe from where …"

"From where you are from," Growly had finished. Ember's eyes were full of tears and he had hugged her tightly, not wanting to say goodbye as the others strapped on their packs.

"Haven *is* my home, Growly." She sniffed, wiping her eyes with the sleeve of her coat. "But …"

"I'll be watching as we travel," he had told her. And as they pushed northward through the blizzard, he had been looking for any firelight or sign of a campsite. So far there had been nothing.

"There are legends of other villages. Just legends though," Breckin had told him. "Maybe they could be somewhere in the north. It is a wild and dangerous place, all cliffs and thundering water and jagged rocks and ice. We have never seen bears there or found a way to travel past the river and the rocks, but there are strange writings near the cliffs. Someone must have made them."

Strange writings? C.J. would want to check on that, but there was a lot to do before then. The first thing was making it safely through this blizzard.

They had come out on the ridge now. The land dropped away to the right, sloping down steeply to the tops of trees far below. The wind howled along the hilltop, kicking up the icy snow in a stinging spray. Chippy was just ahead of him, barely visible in all the swirling snow. Growly could hear his faint muffled shout in his ears. He was tugging on the rope. Just then, a deep, creaking sound filled Growly with alarm.

"Chippy, step back," he cried, leaping to the left as the rope jolted tightly. There was a loud crack as the rope pulled him off his feet and the ice gave way underneath him.

Growly tumbled through the air, thumping over chunks of ice and snow until, with a crash, he thudded into a large rock on the side of the slope. The rope swung out below him, the weight of his two friends and their packs knocking the breath out of him and wedging him hard against the rock. It was just for a moment though. The rope swung wildly to the left and then there was a loud snap. The weight on the rope was gone.

"Chippy!" Growly cried. "Breckin!"

He was pulling desperately on the rope, which was coming back up to him quickly and easily. It had broken. He could see the tattered end of it now. And as he called out for his friends over and over, there was no reply.

He had fallen about halfway down the slope. Looking up, Growly could see the icy shadow of the ridge though the snow, and below him, he could see the tops of the trees at the edge of the forest. His whole body ached, especially his ribs, but at least it didn't seem that anything was broken.

The slope was very steep—parts of it almost straight down. Growly leaned against the rock for a moment, unbuckling his backpack and holding it in front of him with his back against the rock. He had another length of rope inside, and soon he had knotted the two pieces together and had tied one end of the rope to his pack. With his backpack secure, Growly lowered it carefully downward, until he felt it gently land on the snow far below.

"Ok now, slowly," he whispered to himself. He moved easily downward, with the icy rope sliding though his gloved paws as he pushed against the cliff with his boots.

"Breckin! Chippy!" he called out, even as he slid down the slope at the foot of the cliff, looking in every direction for any sign of his friends. He found Chippy first, crumpled up against a tall oak tree, which he had rolled into after hitting the snow. The young monkey looked dazed and dizzy, and like he was in a lot of pain.

"Breckin!" he groaned. "Growly ... his rope ..."

Growly could see Chippy's rope was cut and frayed, with no sign of the Cub anywhere.

"He fell and swung," Chippy groaned again. "That way. Rope snapped." He pointed off to the left. "Then the ground broke and I fell too."

Growly knelt by his friend. "Do you think you can walk, Chippy?"

Chippy nodded, looking for a moment at his left arm. "My shoulder."

Growly dug into his pack, pulling out a wide bandage from his emergency kit.

"I'm going to put it in a sling. It might hurt a little while I tighten it. But it will feel better after that. It *will* make handstands much more difficult though!" he added with a smile.

Chippy gave Growly a tired grin, and then he gasped as the sling was tightened. It did help though.

"Better," Chippy said thankfully, as Growly helped him to his feet. "I can carry my pack on one shoulder. Till we find Breckin."

They set off along the cliff face, moving slowly so they wouldn't risk missing him in the heavy snow. It wasn't long before they came across a line of flattened snow, rolling down over another slope and into the trees.

"Breckin!" Growly cried, bounding down the steep hillside with Chippy close behind. The markings in the snow continued downward for a short way, and then disappeared over another drop.

"Breckin!" Growly cried again. And this time there was a groan from somewhere down below. Growly crawled to the edge of the drop, peering down to a frozen riverbed where the battered Cub lay amongst old leaves and clumps of snow.

"Growly!" he groaned, and a weak smile spread across his face. "I knew that you would …" His voice trailed off to a whisper as his eyes slowly closed.

16
Unexpected Visitors

Growly strained to keep his balance as they came down another hill, crunching through the deep snow with the stretcher dragging close behind. Chippy was at his side, dragging a stretcher of his own with the three companions' backpacks tied securely between the poles.

Growly looked over at Chippy with a strained smile, and Chippy did his best to smile too, though Growly could see that the monkey's shoulder was causing him a lot of pain.

"Keep going," Chippy shouted, before Growly could even ask if they needed to stop. "Breckin needs help ... doctor."

Growly nodded. From the moment they had found him it was obvious that the Cub was badly hurt. His leg was already swollen, and there were many scrapes and bruises on his arms and body. They had made a splint for his leg and bandaged up the scrapes as best as possible, but Breckin was still unconscious and would need more help than they could give him.

Chippy had the idea for the stretcher. The monkeys used them to help haul fruit when they were out in the jungles around Towerwood. They were made of two long poles, joined together by ropes and netting. In this case, they had used Growly's sleeping bag, attaching it to the poles with bindings from his pack. They had made a harness, which Growly wore over his shoulders, and placed Breckin in the sleeping bag, wrapped warmly in his extra coat and his scarf pulled high under his hood. The stretcher slid easily over the snow, though it was still heavy, especially going up the hills.

They had made good distance on the first day, pushing through the blizzard winds as they made their way through the trees. At times they stopped to check on Breckin, sheltering in a shallow cave or hollow and putting their ears close to listen to his breathing. Sometimes he moaned, as if he were dreaming, and once Growly thought he was almost about to open his eyes, but mostly the Cub looked feverish and frail.

Both Growly and Chippy had decided to continue walking through the night, in the hope that they might soon find someone from Breckin's village. Perhaps some scouts or bears out foraging. They had to try.

Now, as the first morning light brightened the woods around them, Growly began to wonder if perhaps they might have pushed too hard. Chippy's face was strained and exhausted, and he was gasping with every step. And Growly could feel his whole body aching, his legs wobbling and quivering and hardly

able to move. "We need to rest," Growly gasped. "I …
just for a moment."

Chippy was too exhausted to even answer. He just
gave a weak nod, stumbling for a moment in the snow.

"Over there!" Growly shouted, his voice croaky
and sore. He pointed over to a small hollow,
underneath an overhanging rock. It was not a cave,
but it did provide some shelter from the wind. "Just a
couple of hours sleep, and then we can get moving."

Growly and Chippy placed Breckin's stretcher
between them, laying on either side in their sleeping
bags under the overhanging rock. There was no place
to build a fire, and they had no strength to make one.
As they lay down on the hard, cold ground, they
quickly fell to sleep.

"Wake up! Growly!" Chippy's voice was full of
alarm and it shook Growly from his troubled dreams.

He could feel a drift of snow piled up against his
back, and as he blearily opened his eyes he saw in an
instant why Chippy had awakened him. Breckin was
missing! His sleeping bag lay open on the stretcher,
with a light dusting of snow over the place where he
had been.

Growly scrambled from under the shelter, kicking
up a shower of snow as he staggered to his feet. His
body ached terribly, and his muscles were stiff and
cramped. He hardly thought about it though, as he

looked for any sign of where Breckin might have been taken.

Taken? The thought was a shock to Growly, even as it came into his mind. Who would take him? It didn't make sense, but where else could he be?

"Look Growly," Chippy shouted. He was pointing to markings in the snow, already almost covered by the blizzard and the wind.

There were boot prints heading down a slope, with a line from something being dragged. Breckin's splinted leg. Growly could see at once the Cub had ventured out into the woods.

Chippy was already moving, following the trail for a short distance until, suddenly he dropped to the ground behind a large boulder, turning back to Growly with his eyes wide in astonishment.

"Growly!" he gasped. He was trying to find the words to say, but his mouth just trembled, whispering something in Monkey.

Growly was still a little way behind, but as he came up closer and peered though the heavy snow, he gasped, tumbling down next to Chippy before he slowly crept out again to peek around the rock.

"H … H … Horses!" Chippy stammered, finally finding the word he had been looking for.

Down in a hollow among the trees, Breckin stood with his arms around the neck of a tall, brown horse, surrounded by many others throughout the trees.

"It's hurt!" Growly said in dismay. "Breckin must

be trying to help it. Look at the branches tangled on its head!"

Chippy gasped. The monkey had loved horses ever since he had met them trapped in the Alps and had promised that he would rescue them one day. He had not expected to find horses here though.

"We have to help!" Growly said. "Look, many of them are hurt, all tangled up in branches. How could it have happened?"

They crept out from behind the boulder, walking slowly and carefully toward Breckin so as not to scare the injured creatures. "They seem to like Breckin," Growly whispered. "Perhaps they know he can help. Now walk very carefully, Chippy."

"Growly! Chippy!" Breckin's shout made Growly jump, and Chippy let out a squeal.

There was sudden movement all around Breckin, with hoofbeats and snorts and long legs kicking up the snow. The horse that Breckin was holding didn't move though. He just gazed up at Growly and Chippy as they came closer, gently nodding his head.

"Breckin!" Growly gasped. "Are you?" He put his paw to Breckin's head. It was hot and feverish, and Growly could see the Cub was in a lot of pain.

"*We* can help them," Growly said, nodding to the animals all around. "*You* need to rest. You are very sick."

"Help them? What do you mean?" Breckin suddenly looked very confused.

"The horses," Growly replied, trying to speak

slowly in case Breckin was too sick to understand. "Chippy and I can help the horses. All the injured ones stuck in the branches ..." Growly's voice trailed off as he looked more closely at the horse Breckin was holding on to. It looked like the branches were growing right out of its head. His heart began to pound in alarm. This was far more serious that he had first thought.

Chippy saw it too, and he let out a cry, holding Growly tightly by the arm as he pointed in dismay. "He's hurt, Growly! What will we do?"

Breckin watched them both in confusion. Horses? Help them?

"They're here to help *us*," Breckin said after a moment. "And what are horses?"

"B ... b ... but the branches!" Chippy stammered, pointing to the animal's head.

"The antlers?" Breckin said. He was finally beginning to understand. "This ... this is a deer!"

They had come while Growly and Chippy were sleeping.

Breckin had awakened in the midst of his fever to their calls a little way off in the woods. He didn't know why he had stumbled off into the blizzard. Perhaps it was the fever, but something told him that the three of them were in a lot of trouble, and he must try to find help while it was close by. Dragging his splinted leg behind him, he had shuffled down into the clearing, finding the herd of deer among the trees.

"Deer have always been friendly to the bears of Arborstone," Breckin explained to an astonished Growly and Chippy. "We know a little of the way they talk. I was asking for help."

And now they were moving quickly through the forest, with Breckin's stretcher pulled by one of the larger bucks, and Growly and Chippy riding close beside. Chippy had his arms wrapped tightly around the strong animal's neck, and he had a excited grin spread across his face. These strange animals might not be horses, but they were just as wonderful to him. Another deer dragged the stretcher with their backpacks, moving quickly through the snow at a steady trot.

As night fell, they continued northwestward, moving out over some open land and then back into the woods. The deer seemed to have no trouble in the darkness, grunting and snorting to each other to keep from getting lost.

And then, sometime in the early hours, the herd came suddenly to a stop, the larger buck letting out a loud cry in the darkness. Just up ahead, down a long slope through the snow, the orange glow of firelight flickered in amongst the trees.

17

Arborstone

Growly slid off the back of the buck he had been riding, feeling his boots sink deep into the soft, powdery snow. The firelight was just through the trees, and he thought he could hear the sound of snoring, even above the whistle of the wind. He would go in alone, so as not to cause alarm. Breckin was asleep again, restless and feverish, and Chippy ... well ... Breckin had assured them a monkey was quite an astonishing thing for an Arborstone bear to see.

Stepping through the trees, Growly came upon a rough campsite, with three small tents and an open fire with brightly glowing coals. And there, sitting by the fireside was a warmly bundled bear, looking up at Growly in surprise. Growly stepped quickly into the firelight, crouching down next to the seated bear and holding out is paw.

"Growly," he said, as if that might help explain things. The astonished bear took his paw, shaking it as he continued to stare with his mouth half open. "I ...

I'm Orley," he mumbled, still not sure if this might be a dream.

He was a fairly young bear, Growly could tell, perhaps just a little older than he was, with light, caramel colored fur under his heavy coat.

"I have injured friends," Growly said quickly. "A friend of mine and a bear named Breckin. Do you know him?"

"Breckin!" Orley jumped to his feet, shouting out to the bears who had been sleeping in the tents. "Breckin! Breckin's here! Everyone. Hurry up!"

There was a scramble of activity. Shouts and calls of bears stumbling out of their tents. Orley was already disappearing into the trees, calling out in joy as he found the waiting deer. "It *is* him! It's Breckin and a Little Cub I think ... Oh my!"

Growly heard a happy, familiar laugh and then, "Chippy! I'm a monkey."

A lot happened then. Breckin was carried into the camp, and Chippy stumbled in beside Orley, who had already decided he loved these things called monkeys, whatever they might be. Bears rushed here and there, gathering supplies and medicines, all the while trying to catch another glimpse of Chippy, who sat by the fire.

The bears were a scouting team, and they had been out in the woods for two weeks now continuing the search for Breckin, which had been going on ever since it was known he was missing. "There are teams out all over the Widelands," Orley had told them, "searching for three things: help, food, and Breckin. And now, all those things have found us. You say there are stockpiles in your village, Growly?"

Growly nodded. "We have food stored in the Westwind Caverns and in the storecaves throughout Haven. Enough for the winter for all of us, I think, if we are careful."

One of the other bears looked up from where he had been kneeling next to Breckin. "We should leave soon," he said seriously. He had just finished changing Breckin's bandages and was giving him some kind of syrup. "It will help with the fever. At least till we get there."

The tents were quickly packed, and soon they were on their way, with the deer helping haul Breckin's stretcher and carry the bears so they could travel more quickly. Growly was amazed to see Orley and his friends communicate with the large creatures. It was not a conversation, really, but the bears could make sounds a lot like the deer, and the deer seemed to answer in reply.

They traveled quickly through the early morning hours, watching the sun come up behind them in the east. It was just a dull glow, as the snow was still falling, but the wind had gotten calmer and the clouds seemed less bleak.

They spent the day pushing on through the forests, stopping to eat for dinner in a cave by a frozen creek. Then it was back into the forest, on into the night with just their lamps to show the way. It was the deer who kept them going in the right direction.

"All deer know about Arborstone," Orley had said. "They often come to see it in the spring and summer, and in the winter we feed them if they have trouble finding food. I thought every bear would know about deer." Orley was thoughtful for a moment before he continued. "Well, I didn't know about horses ... or monkeys! I would truly love to see a horse one day, Chippy," he had added with a smile.

It was sunrise when they first saw it—a bright, twinkling sparkle far in the distance through the trees. Chippy saw it first. He had been awake, thinking about Annily, and at first he thought it might just be sunlight on the snow. As they continued on though, the twinkling got wider and wider, and the sparkle reminded him of something from his home.

"Water!" he cried, looking over at Growly as he shouted it again. "Water! Water!" And it was. Before them was an enormous stretch of water, as far as the eye could see.

They came out on a snow covered beach, with boulders and rocky outcrops to the north and the south. Huge chunks of ice floated out in the water, like slowly moving mountains drifting down toward the south. The water was clear and blue and sparkling, even with the dark clouds and snow—a blue that went on and on until it disappeared from sight.

It was not the Ocean, at least as far as the history books would say. It had not been anywhere near this big in Hegel's day, though it had still been very big. *"Across the Salington Sea lie wonders beyond the wildest dreams."* But even in Hegel's day, no bear had any clue what those wonders might happen to be. The bears of Haven had read about it in Hegel's writings, but seeing it now, Growly could hardly believe his eyes. If this wasn't the Ocean, it might as well be. It would take a special boat to cross an enormous stretch of water like this. A Chippy boat, Growly thought to himself with a smile.

As the sun rose higher, they made their way northward along the beach, going back into the woods at times when they encountered difficult, rocky places. Chippy sat high as he rode along, looking out in wonder at the sparkling water. There had been many times he had been afraid out on the Ocean, but there was a quiet majesty about these sparkling waters and the slowly drifting ice. It reminded him of something his mother used to say when they would sit on the beach looking out over Towerwood Lake, talking about thoughts and ideas in the summer evening warmth. "Still waters run deep, Chipington." He thought then that she was talking about the lake. But she always said it looking at him, and she always said it in a quiet, gentle voice. "You're a tender, quiet soul, little monkey, but you'll find a way to let all those wonderful ideas come out."

There were many deer traveling with them. Now that they were out of the trees, Chippy could see there were at least fifty, and more were joining them as they went along. The lead buck let out a bellowing call from time to time, and as the day wore on, more deer came from the forest.

Breckin was doing a little better. The medicine had helped, and now he rode alertly on the stretcher, talking to those around him and staring out wistfully at the water. He was recognizing landmarks now: Broken Arch, the Tree Stump Beach, the Speckled Islands. They were almost home.

Home. Breckin felt his heart sink. It was all gone now. There *wasn't* home any more.

"Arborstone!" Orley shouted. He had been riding out ahead. Now he came galloping back, his deer kicking up the snow and sand under its hoofs. "Arborstone!" he said again, pointing out over the sparkling waters.

Growly had to shade his eyes to see it at first. Out in the middle of a glistening bay stood the roofs and tower tops of what was once a bustling village. There was a forest of trees out in the water, with only the tops of their branches showing, and a tall majestic outcrop of rock from which the village got its name. The towers of some buildings could be seen up above the surface of the water. But all was empty and abandoned, with walkways disappearing down into the water, and brightly painted towers standing lonely and alone.

All of a sudden there was a shout from the nearby forest, and then another and another. Bears were running out onto the beach, cheering and looking at the enormous herd of deer in wonder. More and more bears were coming out onto the beach, hundreds of them, and still they kept coming. Growly looked on in amazement. He knew Arborstone was bigger than Haven, but somehow he hadn't expected *this* big. The crowd now covered most of the beach around them, pressing in to see who it was riding on the deer.

"This is Growly!" Orley shouted, "He has come to help us. From his village across the Great River."

There were gasps of wonder as the bears pressed even closer so they could see.

Suddenly someone caught sight of Chippy, and shouted in astonishment. "A Little Cub!"

Chippy grinned, and Orley smiled proudly. "Not this one," he said, patting Chippy kindly on the shoulder "He's a monkey, and he's a friend."

18
A Gathering of Bears

"We sent scouts out in all directions," Orley was saying, as he led Growly and Chippy into the trees. Tents and rough shelters were set up under the branches, and wisps of smoke rose out of the narrow caves amongst the rocks. Snow was everywhere, piled high beside paths and walkways throughout the encampment.

"The scouts went out as soon as Arborstone flooded. We knew we must find help if we could, or more food and supplies. It was late in the season for foraging, and much of our stores were washed away in the flood. We're already running low, and the snow has just begun."

Growly could see the bears were in great trouble. Their shelters were barely holding up against the wind and snow, and their clothes were worn and ragged from the rough conditions in the woods. They wore warm smiles on their faces though, and their eyes were full of hope.

Everyone was already hard at work, gathering

belongings, packing clothes and supplies, and preparing what would be left behind. Not much could be taken on the journey southward, so what was saved from the flooding would be packed up in the caves, to be stored until a later time.

Growly and Chippy walked with Orley through the encampment, followed by a noisy bustle of well over one hundred Cubs. All of them wanted to get a closer look at Chippy. The truth is, *everyone* did. It was wonderful that strangers had arrived with the hope of rescue. But none of them could have ever imagined a stranger quite like this.

Chippy wished he could do a handstand, but his arm was still tied up in the sling. It wasn't broken though. The lead doctor of Arborstone had assured him of this. "A dislocated shoulder," he had said and had quickly set it back in place, though it still was very, very sore.

"He's just down this way," Orley said as they came to a ragged tent, barely holding together in the whistling wind. He should have had a better place, but we were running out of tents and …"

"Hello!" A tall, burly bear suddenly stepped out of the tent, startled to see Growly, and then, astonished at the sight of Chippy, "… and … hello!"

He looked at the monkey for a long, thoughtful moment, his face slowly lighting up in a smile full of wonder.

Suddenly he stuck both his paws out, one to Growly and the other to Chippy. "My name is

Umberton. Head of the Rescue Committee and *temporary* mayor of Arborstone. You've already met my son, Breckin." He gave them a wink as they clumsily shook his paws. The *real* mayor of Arborstone is out foraging in the woods. Now that is a *true* mayor. Wise, kind, discerning, beautiful," Umberton grinned.

"And your wife!" Orley finished.

Umberton smiled kindly at Orley, and gave Growly and Chippy another wink.

"She knows foraging like no other, and so she is out with a large team. There is still some food to be found in these woods. Scouts have been sent to find her, from the moment you arrived. Now, Growly is it? And, Chippy? If you don't mind, the Elders are waiting now to meet you."

It was the next morning when they all stood out on the beach. Hundreds upon hundreds of bears, with as many deer between them. Quite a few of the deer were harnessed to sleighs. It was a tradition they had followed for centuries, helping the bears of Arborstone haul supplies in from the woods. Other deer were carrying bundles, and the young deer carried Cubs. The bears themselves had walking poles and rolled up tents and packs.

Umberton's wife, Arien, had returned the night before, along with a group of the northern scouts who had been making their way back home. One of them,

Balliwick, now stood beside Growly and Chippy, answering their many questions about what he had seen far up in the north.

"Yes, yes, I know of the writings, Growly. I've seen them a few times before. But it's not Bear. We had copied it all in our library, out there," he said sadly, nodding toward the sunken ruins. "It's all gone now."

"Is there any of it you remember?" Growly asked. Perhaps the writings could be connected to whoever started the fire Ember had seen in the spring. He was wondering if the words might be some long forgotten type of Old Bear. Perhaps it could be a clue to Ember's home, before she had been found as a Baby Cub on the banks of the Great River.

"Yes, I know a couple of sentences," Balliwick said. "We all learn how to copy a little of it when we're Cubs. Here …"

Balliwick took off his pack for a moment, digging inside for a piece of paper and a pencil. He was just about to start writing when a shout went out from up ahead. It was Umberton. He would continue to lead the bears of Arborstone, at least until they arrived safely in Haven.

"Farewell, Arborstone!" he shouted. "Until the waters go down and we can safely return."

And then they were moving, a long, silent line that stretched back into the woods. No one said a word as they looked out over the water to the ruins of what had once been their home. They had gotten used to the idea that their village was gone. But now, seeing it fall behind them in the biting sleet and snow, a deeper kind of ache seemed to rise up from within them.

Growly could see the sadness on Balliwick's face, and on Orley's, who was walking at Chippy's side.

Taking the pencil and paper gently from Balliwick's paw, he smiled.

"You can show me the writings later. Right now I would like to hear about your adventures in Arborstone. I'm sure it truly is a wonderful place."

Balliwick looked puzzled for a moment, but then a sad smile appeared on his face. "Well, there was the time that Orley got stranded in his canoe and had to be rescued by the rowing team."

Orley looked over at his friend, rolling his eyes and letting out a groan.

"Or the time Balliwick pretended he was a great chef. When he was a Cub. He used *every* ingredient in his mother's kitchen to bake ... what was it Balliwick?"

"Everything pie," Balliwick said, holding back a laugh.

"He made eight of them," Orley chuckled, "and gave one to the mayor."

Now they were both laughing, and those around them were laughing too.

Then a song rose up from the voice of a bear nearby. It was slow and a little sad at first, but in a beautiful way, like the last light of a wonderful day.

Across the golden waters,
And the ruins of Whistiglen,

In the lands now long forgotten,
But by whispers in the wind.
Where the shores stretch quiet and solemn,
As they wait upon a sign,
Of the ones almost forgotten,
By the passing sands of time.

As the verse went on, more and more voices joined in, until the chorus rose up joyfully, echoing out along the beach as the ruins of Arborstone fell behind into the distance.

Oh, across the golden waters,
There are treasures beyond count,
There are treasures that are greater,
Than a very great amount.
There are treasures that are greater,
Than all history has known,
But they cannot touch the treasure,
That's the treasure of my home.

They were all crying as they sang—Growly and Chippy too. But as the song went on, there were smiles amongst the tears, and hope mixed with the sadness. This song was coming with them, along with their stories and memories too. There was a lot that was special about Arborstone that was not being left behind.

They stayed on the beaches as much as they could, looking out over the icy waters as they traveled steadily south. Huge chunks of ice drifted out on the water, and something about it was making Chippy feel uneasy. Bears would point out at the massive bergs from time to time, watching in wonder as they silently drifted by. The Cubs were always excited to see them, pointing with mitten covered paws as they ran along the beach when another came into view.

"There are never this many," Balliwick was saying, "or this size. It's been like this for almost a month. Up to the north, the waterways are jammed with ice and overflowing. Something is happening up there in the mountains."

The words made Chippy shiver, and not because he was cold.

As they made camp that night, the four companions sat around the fire. Chippy had put aside his worried thoughts to sing some monkey songs to the bears gathered around. Breckin was there too, with his broken leg in a cast and his arm freshly bandaged.

"Don't Throw the CoCoNut!" was a favorite with the monkeys of Towerwood, and the bears here loved it too, though he had to stop half way through the song to explain what a coconut is. Breckin sang a few more Arborstone songs, and Orley told some stories from their history.

It was getting late when Growly slid over to Balliwick, handing him the paper and pencil had been carrying in his pocket. "Do you think you could write

those sentences for me now?" Growly asked. "I forgot
to mention it in all the busyness today."

Balliwick smiled. "Now, let me try and remember."
Slowly and carefully he began to make markings on
the paper, stopping occasionally to think before
continuing again. "That's it, I'm sure," he said, "or at
least very close. It may as well be scribbles though. Let
me know what you think."

He handed the paper to Growly, holding it low so
it could be seen in the firelight.

As he took the paper in his paw, Growly let out a
gasp. His mind raced as he looked down at the
markings.

"Chippy! Chippy, look at this paper!" Growly's
paw was shaking and he could hardly keep it still.

The startled monkey took it from Growly's paw.

"The writings, Growly," he cried. "It's … it's
People!"

19
With Thunderhoof & Swift

People. Growly was still amazed as he thought about it. Neither he nor Chippy had been able to read the words, but there was no doubt it was the writing of people. They had seen it a lot in their travels, in paintings and carvings and books.

C.J. would know how to read it. Growly was certain. C.J. knew how to read that language and how to speak it too. But how did *people* writings get all the way up here? He and Chippy had talked about it a little as they traveled, just imagining, really. Growly couldn't help but notice his friend often looked like his thoughts were drifting off somewhere else. Like the ice out on the water.

In fact, it seemed like Chippy's thoughts weren't just like the ice on the water, they were *about* the ice. There were many times when Growly watched him, staring out at the tall shapes as they traveled along, with worry drawn across his face. The monkey did his best not to show his uneasiness, encouraging those around him with stories and songs.

There was a lot to do as they traveled. At the start of each day, scouts would go ahead, moving quickly on deer-back to prepare places to camp and eat. Growly and Chippy helped as much as they could, traveling with the scouts at times and helping with supplies and with the Little Cubs.

On the fourth day of travel, the snowfall finally stopped. Growly awoke to a gentle silence, and the crimson, orange glow of sunrise on the beach. As the other bears awoke, there were happy shouts and cheers as the light of the morning stretched out over the water.

They would begin to head inland today. The Barrier River was just a few miles ahead, and if they traveled at a steady pace, they could reach the tunnel by nightfall. They would camp on this side of the river and cross underneath the following morning.

The woods were full of the sounds of birds, coming out of their shelters after the long, hard days of the blizzard. The deer who weren't carrying supplies or riders leapt about in the glistening snow, bounding through the trees at the edge of the forest. Cubs ran about in all directions, dodging between the branches with snowballs and building snow-bears to watch the trampled trail behind them.

It wasn't long till they could hear the roar of the Barrier River through the trees. Soon they saw the sparkling waters and the churning rapids stretching wide to the other shore far to the south.

The bears at the front started a marching song. It

began with bears chanting deep bass notes and then a call that was shouted out, to which everyone replied. It was a funny song, which seemed to go on and on, and at some points fell apart. But another bear would pick it up again until everyone was singing. After a few times through, Growly was starting to learn the words, and the Cubs around him howled with laughter as he sang at the top of his lungs.

There were other songs sung throughout the afternoon, and it made the time move quickly. Growly even taught those around him "Adventure, My Bear, Adventure," and soon everyone was singing it, though most were getting it wrong. They did sing the chorus correctly though. They sang it with all their might, and that's what really mattered.

Chippy had been doing his best to join in the fun, but Growly couldn't help but notice the far off expression on his face and the sad look in his eyes. At first he thought his friend was just missing his home or Annily or both. But as evening came, and they finally reached the tunnel, Chippy pulled Growly aside, with tears slipping out onto his cheeks.

"I have to go, Growly," he sniffled, looking up earnestly. "When we get to the other side I have to leave."

Growly was shocked. Leave?

"But … what … where to?" Growly was trying to make sense of what Chippy was telling him.

"I have to go that way," he said croakily, pointing back in the direction of the Salington Sea. "Once we cross under the river, I have to go back that way. When I saw the ice. It's so big. And Balliwick said there is so much more ice this year. Growly, what happens when it melts?"

Growly felt a sudden shiver down his back. "Towerwood!" he gasped.

Chippy nodded, looking back at Growly in dismay. "I have to try and find where the ice is going. That's why I have to go."

Growly was quiet for a long moment. "When do we leave?" he asked softly, the corners of his mouth turning in a gentle smile.

Chippy blinked, the worry on his face melting quickly into gratitude.

"The ice is probably going right over The Precipice and melting somewhere else," Growly said encouragingly. "C.J. said he found many rivers and waterfalls in his travels."

"Yes," Chippy nodded. "That's what I hope. The ice looked as if it was heading far to the west."

"Let's rest tonight then, my friend," Growly said, putting his arm over Chippy's shoulder. "Sing some Arborstone songs and eat fresh roasted acorns. And tomorrow, we'll head west. You and me."

Chippy smiled gratefully. "You and me, Growly."

They left at first light, waving goodbye to their new friends before stepping into the cave. Breckin would help the group find the way to Haven from here. The group would travel east till they came to the Great River, and then south till they reached The Precipice.

Growly and Chippy had emptied their packs, taking out extra clothes and unneeded supplies so they could carry extra food. Two deer would travel with them. Balliwick had communicated with them, and it seemed they understood, as they quickly followed close behind Growly and Chippy, down into the caves. They heard the familiar, unsettling rumble again as they went under the river, and the deer snorted and stomped as they went along.

"I understand, my friend," Growly said, patting the deer closest to him as they made their way along. "I don't like having water above me either, and sometimes I don't like it underneath. *Sometimes* I'm not even fond of taking a bath!"

Chippy chuckled, but he picked his pace up a little too. All of them wanted to get out of the tunnel as soon as they possibly could.

"Look, Growly!" Chippy shouted happily as they stepped into a larger cavern. On the other side was the entryway, and beyond that, morning light.

As they came out into the trees, the two friends checked the bindings on their packs and the other supplies that would be carried by the deer. Growly's deer was a large buck named Thunderhoof. At least that is what Growly had named him.

"They have names of their own, but we have never known how to find out," Orley had told them.

"Thunderhoof sounds like a good name though. He sure is big. These deer are happy to help you in any way they can though. They are grateful for the help you are bringing to the bears of Arborstone."

Chippy had already climbed up on the back of the deer who would carry him. "Swift," Chippy said proudly. He had asked Growly for another Bear word that meant fast. He liked the sound of *Swift*.

With the sun rising behind them, they took off into the woods, the deer dashing through the shallow snow and leaping powerfully through the drifts. At times, they came to sprawling evergreen forests, where the the pine trees towered with a blanket of snow clinging to their needles. In these places, it was easier to travel, with the ground underneath more sheltered and clear. Yet you did have to watch out for chunks of snow that often fell from the branches above.

The day wore on, but the deer didn't seem to get tired. They paused occasionally to drink from a stream, or to eat from a stray bush or fern they found in the woods. Then they were ready again, moving steadily westward.

It was well before sunset when they reached the Salington Sea again. They came over a low ridge, and it caught them by surprise. Bright, glistening water sparkled like stars through the dim woods, until they came out on a wide, open beach. It was longer than any beach Growly had seen in his travels, stretching out to the south till it went out of sight, with no rocks or outcrops, no islands or hills.

The water here was filled with choppy waves, blown rough by a wind coming up from the south.

Thunderhoof turned his head back toward Growly, as if to see if he wanted to continue, and Swift looked over and tilted his head. There was a gleam in their eyes, of excitement and adventure.

"Keep going, Growly?" Chippy asked.

Growly nodded, leaning low on Thunderhoof's back.

"To The Precipice," he whispered, patting the stomping deer gently. "But not a step beyond that," he added with a grin.

20
Along the Edge

They rode quickly through the night, the two deer galloping along the open beach with their riders secure and sleeping. Growly and Chippy had tied themselves with harnesses, just like Orley had shown them, and now they slept as the miles hurried by.

The moon was full and bright, flooding the ground in shimmering light. Growly awoke to the sight of tall firs and pines, wrapped in snow with shadows reaching out over the drifts. The beach ahead was snowy and smooth, stretching onward beside the sparkles of light on the glimmering water.

Midnight came and went, and then the early morning hours, as the deer continued southward on their way along the beach. The moon continued its journey too, slowly overhead, until finally a pale glow rose above the forests and the first light of morning peeked out between the trees.

"Growly!" Chippy gasped. The deer had slowed

down to a trot and were moving now with shuffles and stomps.

Growly sat up quickly, rubbing his eyes and then looking around.

"Look Growly! Look!"

Chippy's face was full of wonder as he pointed up ahead.

Growly rubbed his eyes again, to be sure that he was not just imagining what he was seeing.

The air was filled with swirling color, sparkling and dazzling and twisting upward. The light went on for as far as they could see to the west, like a wall of shimmering rainbows stretching out along ...

"The Precipice!" Growly gasped.

He had seen rainbow light like this before, in the spray of the Great Falls as it plummeted down into the the clouds below, and in the snow that was often blown high and sent twirling by the upward winds in the winter.

Chippy slid off the back of Swift, walking into the swirling rainbows.

"Make sure you don't look up too long, Chippy. Where there are rainbows like that, The Precipice will be just beyond."

Chippy turned back to Growly and grinned. He loved The Precipice, even though it kept him from getting home. He loved to go to the Lookout near Growly's cottage and peer out over the swirling clouds below, which stretched out into the distance like an ocean.

Chippy didn't go any closer this time though. He could see the snow whipping up into the air near the edge, and the dangerous black ice glistening on the boulders.

"West now," Chippy said, climbing back onto his deer. "Can we ride, Growly? With the deer it is much quicker."

Growly looked out at the path in front of them. There was a thin strip of land ahead to the west, a line of small hills between the Salington Sea and The Precipice.

Leaning down to Thunderhoof's ear, Growly spoke quietly, pointing out to the snowy hills that stretched out before them. "Will you carry us a little further?"

Thunderhoof seemed to understand. With a nod and a snort he took off again, with Swift following close behind.

As they rode along, Chippy's thoughts were far away, far below the swirling clouds and The Precipice. He had ridden like this once before, through mountain canyons and meadows. The horses! How beautiful they had been. And how sad they had looked as he had climbed away, leaving them trapped and forgotten, as their families had been since the ancient days of Crevan.

"No, not forgotten any more," he whispered to himself. "Someday I will come back and help you find a way out of the mountains." That's what he had promised. And somehow he knew, he would find a way to do it.

The deer thundered over the hard-packed snow, racing up the gentle slopes and galloping down the hills. There were woods in some places. Long, narrow patches of tress that grew short and stunted by the winds from the cliffs. The day wore into night, and night into morning, and the morning brought them into a wider stretch of land. Tall hills rose steeply ahead of them, and sharp, jagged rocks towered up above the snow. There was ice out in the water. Growly could see the shapes of the enormous chunks like islands through the trees.

Chippy looked at Growly with worry. "More ice," he said softly. "Growly, look how big it is!"

Growly was quiet for a minute, looking out toward the water, and then back at his friend.

Slipping off of Thunderhoof's back, Growly dug through one of the bundles on the deer's back and came over to Chippy.

"Come on," he said softly, his face widening in a smile. There is something I've been wanting to show you for a very long time."

"We'll have to walk a little way, but I promise you it will be worth it."

They made their way up the tall hill, trudging upward through the deep snow until they reached the top. The worry had fallen from Chippy's face a little, and now he was mostly wondering what Growly was going to do. There was a joyful gleam in his friends eyes that was starting to make him *very* curious.

"Close your eyes Chippy," Growly said. There was the sound of something unwrapping. Then Growly was helping him to sit, on a blanket … (or part of a tent?) … laid out in the snow.

"Hold on tight," Growly said, putting the edge in Chippy's gloved hands. "Are you ready?"

Chippy didn't know what to say. "Growly? Ready for what?"

All of a sudden they they were moving. Chippy could hear the whooshing sound of snow as they picked up speed. "Open your eyes!" Growly shouted happily, his voice rising up into a happy howl.

Chippy opened his eyes to see he was racing down the hillside, sitting on a large piece of canvas with Growly right behind him. They were getting faster and faster, and now Chippy was shouting happily too, laughing and howling as they went. There were bumps that sent them flying into the air and smooth stretches where they raced across the snow. Then, nearing the bottom of the hill, they came to a steep drop. It felt almost as if they were falling until suddenly they shot up a rise and soared out into the air.

"Growleeeeee! I'm flying!" Chippy howled, his shout mixed with happy laughter. Growly didn't hear him though. He was too busy spinning through the air after falling off the back. They came down with two soft thuds, disappearing beneath the powdery snow before they leaped up again with roars of laughter.

"Again!" Chippy begged. He was completely covered in snow, with just his eyes and mouth showing through the white.

"Of course!" Growly laughed, reaching down to grab the piece of canvas as the two bemused deer watched from nearby.

They continued sliding for another hour, until they both lay gasping contentedly in the snow.

"Chippy," Growly said, looking kindly at his friend. "It's going to be ok. Whatever we find up ahead."

The monkey nodded, looking at Growly with a grateful smile. He felt much better after the fun in the snow. "Thank you, friend," he whispered. "Come on, let's find out."

It was afternoon when they said goodbye to the deer. They had come to a place where the way had grown narrow, just a thin strip of jagged rocky land between the water and The Precipice.

"They will wait here, I think," Growly said. The deer had gone over to a place amongst the trees and were watching the bear and the monkey as they left.

With one last look back, the two friends climbed up into the rocks, making their way slowly as the hours passed by. It was hard to see much. The rocks rose up around them, and they traveled through narrow paths, following the lowering sun. It had almost set when they finally came to a steep, jagged outcrop that blocked the way ahead. They would have to climb.

Growly motioned for Chippy to leave his backpack. "Let's go up and see what's ahead first. Then we can pull them up with ropes."

Chippy nodded. Climbing with packs on this steep, slippery slope could be dangerous.

They inched their way upwards, coming to a tight crevice in the rock, which they crawled through until they slid down the other side. There was another narrow walkway, which went a short way ahead and then curved, disappearing to the right in the blinding light of the sunset.

Just then, they heard a loud, rumbling, groan—a scraping sound that made the earth beneath them tremble.

"Chippy!" Growly cried. "What was that?"

Chippy was already moving down the narrow path. "This way!" he shouted. "We must see! Before it's dark!"

Chippy reached a wide open area, which came to a sudden stop just up ahead of him.

"Chippy!" Growly shouted, as he saw the danger. "Wait! It's a cliff!"

Chippy skidded to a stop, looking around in alarm, suddenly realizing what it was he was seeing. Huge walls of ice towered up into the air, and behind them more and more, as far as he could see out into the lake. The cliff ahead was where a waterfall once

flowed, now blocked by the walls of ice which scraped
and groaned against each other.

"The falls!" Growly gasped as he came up next to
Chippy, peering over the edge into the clouds far
below.

Chippy didn't look up, and his voice was just a
whisper as he nodded. "The falls, Growly … and …
Towerwood."

21
Ember & Annily

mber stepped out of the cave into bright morning sunlight, which glistened through the spray that hung like mist in the air. All around, bears were running with cables and ropes, their breath puffing out like steam and drifting off behind them in the cold. It was a very different place now than the day they first arrived. Wooden shelters were scattered throughout the clearing, with more in the process of being built. There were tents too, many of them.

Ember strolled through the busyness toward a tall tower which had been built amongst the trees. The cable hung taut and secure now, stretching out across the river to another tower, far, far away on the other side.

"Good morning Ember!" came a joyful voice. It was Pepper, chief engineer Ruslan's daughter. She had come to the island a couple of days after Ember, inching her way over the rope with just a harness to hold her in place. Ten bears had come that day, all of them engineers, and they had all hauled the cable across in the following days with pulleys and winches. Once the cable was in place, more bears had come, and now there were over fifty. All the while the eagles had also been helping carry over supplies.

"Pepper!" Ember smiled, putting her arm around the Cub's shoulder to give her a hug. "I slept in this morning after a late night. How is the cable carriage coming?"

Pepper grinned. "Prepared and ready ... with every luxury imaginable," she said in a proper sounding voice, like a poet or the mayor when he was giving a speech. "The *carriage* is ready for the most distinguished of guests. We even added a library for you, my dear, in case you get bored on your journey across the river!"

Ember laughed and rubbed Pepper affectionately on the head. "If only that were true! I haven't read a book in at least two weeks!"

The *carriage*, as it was called, was really just a big, wooden container, with rough benches and high walls. It could carry ten bears at a time, or *perhaps* fifteen, but fifteen would be too much of a risk with the wild river winds. There were also zip lines stretching out over the water, ten of them starting from high in the treetops of the island to landing platforms on the far shore.

Annily was already awake, kneeling by an open fire with pancakes on a griddle. As she saw Ember she waved, motioning for Ember and Pepper to come and join her for breakfast. Ember was just about to sit down when there was a shout from up on the tower. It was Ash, and he was pointing out toward the west.

"Fire!" he was shouting. "Smoke! Look!"

Ember jumped to her feet, running toward a platform that had a telescope in place.

It *was* a fire. Ember could see the thin trail of smoke rising up above the distant trees. It was hard to see that far from here, even with the telescope. But there was no doubt it was smoke.

Ember leapt off the platform, waving to Annily and Pepper to follow as she started running.

Annily was right behind her, still holding the plate with fresh pancakes.

"Where are we going?" Pepper shouted, taking off after Ember and Annily. As she came up beside the monkey, she grabbed a pancake from the wobbling plate. "To help me run faster," she said with a grin.

Ember disappeared down into the cave, where she had been sleeping the night before. It was the entrance to the tunnel Growly and Chippy had left through weeks before.

The friends stopped in the middle of the large cavern, as Ember and Annily went to get lanterns from their packs. "Will you wait and tell the others where we have gone, Pepper?" Ember said to the Cub. "We won't go far on the other side. Just to where the smoke is."

"I'll look after the pancakes Annily," Pepper grinned.

They were just about to go when a there was an

echo from up ahead and a burst of light from down in the tunnel. Suddenly, a large, stout bear came up into the cavern, followed by a line of many others, all carrying lamps. There was a gasp and a moment of stunned silence. Then the bears erupted in joyful shouts and cheers. "Haven!" some shouted. "We're here!"

More and more bears flooded up into the cave, waving their lamps excitedly, some with tears in their eyes. Ember could see they all looked tired and dirty, and many had jackets that were scuffed and torn.

The larger bear stepped forward, a tired smile stretched across his face.

"I'm Umberton," he said. "It is wonderful to see you!"

"Pancakes?" Pepper smiled, holding out the plate, and there were cheers all round the room.

They were a scouting party of twenty, led by Umberton and others of the Arborstone Rescue Committee. They had gone ahead into the tunnel to make sure it was still safe and to see what the next step would be, now that they had made it to the island.

Ember had expected Growly and Chippy might be with this group, but when she didn't see them, she guessed they must be helping back on the other side. She had felt her heart drop at first, when the last of the group came out into the cavern. But it would be alright. It wouldn't be long at all till he was here and they could talk again. Oh how she had missed him. And poor Annily. She was to be married to Chippy …

that is, when they finally got home again. It was so hard for her. Ember and Annily had both talked a lot during their time together on the island.

"He'll be coming over soon, I'm sure," Ember said encouragingly when she saw the sad look on Annily's face.

They led Umberton and his team up onto the island where all the bears of the construction team were beginning to assemble. There were cheers and hugs and shouts of joy and amazement when the Arborstone bears saw what had been built. There was room enough for everyone on the island, with many shelters in place and a large stockpile of tents— enough to house the bears of Arborstone until their turns on the zip lines or in the carriage. Ruslan wanted to start moving bears across the river right away. More bad weather was coming slowly from the west.

There was not much for Ember and Annily to do, so they decided to go and wait down in the cavern for the next group of bears that would soon arrive. A messenger had traveled back as soon as Umberton and his team had come up onto the island, and that was over an hour ago.

It wasn't long until they heard the sound of voices, and the light of lamps appeared from down in the tunnel. Bear after bear climbed up into the cavern, their faces dirty but beaming happily at the sight of

Ember and a monkey. They all rushed excitedly onward, eager to see the sunlight after the darkness of the tunnel.

One Little Cub though tottered over to Annily, throwing his paws around her and squealing, "Monkey!"

The Little Cub's mother, who had been watching with a joyful smile, put her arm around Annily's shoulder and said, "He *loves* monkeys! We all do."

"Chippy?" Annily blurted out. She couldn't hold it in any longer. "Have you met him? Is he coming soon?"

The bear's eyes suddenly seemed troubled, and she stood back for a moment, looking knowingly at Annily, "*Oh* … you must be Annily. He spoke of you before … before he left."

Ember gasped, and Annily's eyes went wide, "He … he *left*?"

The bear nodded. "He and Growly. It was something very important. About his village. They said it should only take them a few days."

Ember felt her heart sink even lower. In a moment she took a deep breath, sniffling a little as she said, "It must have been important then, Annily. Come on. We'll be needed to help set up the tents."

Bears were already ascending into the tower, and others were heading out toward the zip lines in the trees. They would not all get across today though, or tomorrow or the next day. There would be equipment checks and safety precautions, as well as the moving of provisions and supplies. It would take a long time to move a whole village across the Great River.

Ember set her mind on preparing the tents, trying not to think about Growly and Chippy, or the dark clouds in the sky west of the river.

Bears came through the tunnel all that morning, with a pause just after lunch so digging work could be done. The narrow places needed to be widened and the low places made higher for some of the frail bears to more easily get through.

Night fell on a crowded island, with blazing campfires surrounded by singing and laughing amidst the raging roar of the river.

At dawn, the zip lines started again, whizzing out over the river from the tops of the trees. The carriage crept out high on the cable, filled with load after load of very nervous bears.

On the third morning the storm hit, starting first with a strong wind and then a blinding swirl of snow. Most of the bears were across the river by now, and half the engineers had already made the trip back to the other side."

We can't stay too much longer," Ruslan said. "Once the wind picks up again, there will be no more trips across the river. We're getting the last of the Arborstone bears across now. Two more trips in the carriage, I think." His face was stern and serious as he added, "One last look, Ember, but then it will be up to Farren and the Rescue Committee. They're still out there looking."

Ember nodded. "Come on Annily," she said running back to the tunnel for one more look.

They came out on the Golden Floor, like they had the last three days, looking for any sign of Growly and Chippy. Everywhere was swirling snow and wind now. Ember put her paw up to her eyes trying to see any sign of movement out on the rock.

"There's something different! Ember, that wasn't there before!" Annily gasped, pointing out at a small mound of boulders with a few bare branches in between. "It's … it's moving!"

Ember watched in shock as part of the pile of boulders rose higher and higher, and she saw, caught on the branches … a bear!"

"Growly!" she cried, racing over toward him with Annily right behind. It was an animal, Ember could see, now that she was closer, and Growly was holding onto its neck with the last of his strength. And Chippy! He lay with his eyes closed and his leg wrapped in a bandage, with the other animal laying next to him, trying to keep him warm.

22

Recovery

rowly awoke to the sound of laughter in the hallway, as the door opened and someone entered the room. He felt far away and foggy, but the voice sounded somehow familiar, like a voice he had heard when he was a Little Cub. In his jumbled thoughts, he tried to find the last thing he remembered. Chippy had fallen … he was bleeding … and they had to shelter near the cliffs. He had awakened with a fever, and Chippy still unconscious. He remembered carrying his friend, snow and everything feeling blurry … and horses … no … deer. Then nothing after that.

"Growly." There was the voice again. It seemed a little louder this time.

Growly fought his way out of the fogginess. It took all of his effort to slowly open his eyes.

It was Dr. Umika, sitting at the foot of his bed with a look of great relief on her face.

"Oh Growly, you wouldn't believe how good it is to see you with your eyes open," she sighed. "Your fever broke last night, but after so long we all knew your body must be weak."

So long? Growly looked at Dr. Umika in confusion. "How ... how long have I been here?"

"About two weeks, Growly," she said softly. "We'd tried about everything except Aventhistle, and I was starting to consider that. There are two monkeys and a lot of worried bears out there in the hall ... and all throughout Haven and the Westwind Caverns."

"Chippy?" Growly whispered. He was finding it hard to speak, and he could feel tiredness sweeping over him again.

"Chippy is doing fine, though I do wish he would rest more. He hobbles along through Haven with Annily and Ember and their friends. He has a cast, and some bumps and scrapes on his head, but you would hardly know it by the way he gets around. Now, I have some medicine and a little soup here for you, if you can eat some. Now that the fever is broken, we have to help get your strength back."

In the weeks that followed, Growly continued to get stronger, moving quickly from weak broth and herb tea to vegetables and stews. (Not to mention an enormous apple pie that his mother baked, which was shared by friends and family that packed into his room.) As his strength returned, Growly started to venture out into a house that was full of the bustle and activity of many bears.

Umberton and his family were staying with them now, along with another family who was living in the storage cave next to the kitchen. Every home in Haven was filled with Arborstone families, and there were hundreds more bears living down in the Westwind Caverns.

"From the day you left for Heflin's Reach, we were working in preparation," Growly's mother told him, "making mattresses and blankets and gathering spare clothes, which we stored in the library. We have rationed supplies, and with the emergency food from the storage caves, I believe we can all make it safely through this winter."

There was still much to be done. Every day, teams went out into the Lower Woods to search for extra food. Others were bringing down supplies from Glider Leap or from the tunnels near the broken River Gates at the top of the Backland Valley. Everything took longer in the snow, but there were many bears now to do the work.

In the evenings, there were gatherings throughout the village, in the Town Hall and the Library, the Lookout and the Westwind Caverns. Haven bears and Arborstone bears shared stories and songs, laughing and learning about each other's histories. It was one of Growly's favorite times of the day, and as more weeks passed by he came to love the bears of Breckin's village.

As Growly's strength returned, his bedroom was transformed, with beds for Chippy and Breckin, who had been sleeping in the living room. The three friends talked long into the night. Breckin was fascinated with stories about the monkeys of Towerwood and the others Growly and Chippy had encountered in their travels.

"How many do you think there are?" he asked one night, his eyes wide with wonder as Growly told about Seaward Bluff, the City of Monkeys.

"Thousands and thousands," Chippy had told him. He had been shocked when he first saw it too. "And many, many more scattered all throughout the islands."

"Thousands!" Breckin whispered, trying to imagine a place so wonderful. "Oh Chippy, I would so love to see it one day!"

"When the path is opened back down The Precipice, I'm going to visit Chippy's home," Growly said. "Perhaps one day you might see the monkey city too."

Chippy had gone quiet as Growly mentioned The Precipice, and soon the conversation had moved on to other things. But Chippy's thoughts were far away, and worry was creeping it's way back in.

A few days later, they were out in the village early with Annily and Ember and many of their friends.

Gittel had prepared a picnic backpack, and Ash and Skye were loaded down with small sleds.

It was a beautiful day, with clear skies and a bright sunrise creeping up over The Precipice—the perfect day for sledding down by Growly's cottage in the hidden meadow.

Bears were staying there, two families from Arborstone, and Growly and the others had supplies for them loaded in their packs.

"Make sure these pies get there safely!" Growly's grandmother, Edolie, had told them with a wink. I wouldn't want one to go *missing* on the way!"

And so they set off, making their way along the zig-zagging path that led down the Little Cliffs, and out over the snowy meadows of the Lower Lands. Finally they came to the narrow pass and through the patch of trees that opened into the Hidden Meadow.

As they came closer they could see smoke rising from the chimney of the cottage, and there were three Little Cubs playing out on the swing. When they saw Growly and his friends, they squealed with delight, clambering through the snow to ride on their shoulders and to hold Chippy and Annily's hands.

Once the supplies were delivered, it was time for sledding, starting at the top of a slope near the back porch of the cottage and catching speed down the steep slope to a place near The Precipice. There was a small lookout there, where Growly had often gone as a Cub, gazing out over the clouds and wondering what might be below. He knew now—or at least a little of it.

There was a whole world out there, with wonderful creatures like Annily and Chippy. And there was Towerwood.

"Growly," Chippy said quietly. They were standing near the Lookout, waiting for the Cubs to have their turn on the sleds, just in case they had trouble slowing down.

Growly looked at his friend. There was worry in the monkey's voice.

"It's the digging, isn't it?" Growly said. "The report from Ruslan?"

Chippy nodded. "The ground will still be too hard to dig, for us to change the Cascade and get to Towerwood in time."

"Yes," Growly said seriously. He had been thinking about it too. When the ice started moving again back at the falls, it would already be too late.

"I've tried to think of other ways. Perhaps we go back to the falls. Perhaps there is a way down there, maybe. Oh Growly, I don't know *what* to do." Tears began to trickle down the monkey's cheeks. Chippy didn't even wipe them away. He just looked at at Growly helplessly.

Growly put his paw on Chippy's shoulder, not saying anything for a moment. He could could feel a sick, frightened feeling deep in his stomach at the words he knew he was about to say next.

"There might be another way, Chippy, but it's dangerous, and it has never been tried."

23
Over the Edge

Skye stood next to Annily on the platform, with her arm around the worried monkey's shoulders as she tried her best to sound encouraging.

"It's just a test," she said assuringly ... as assuringly as she could. No one really knew what was about to happen next.

"And the snow is soft here," Ember added. "Just in case."

Gittel was hard at work, checking bindings and straps to make sure everything was ready. At least as ready as you could be for something that had never been tried before.

They were at the top of a hill, on a tall platform which had been built for this purpose. Built of rough boards, it was quite wide and long, with enough room for five or six bears. And the glider of course. Never in the history of Haven had there been a glider quite like this.

It was part of the plan Farren and Growly had talked about long ago, before he left across the river with Breckin and Chippy. C.J. had been there too. It was his idea from the beginning. He had a way of thinking of things that were always a little bit different, and sometimes a little bit dangerous. "There would be many risks," he had said, "but it just could work, of course *only* if there aren't any other options." C.J. had shown them sketches and calculations. Just the thought of it had made Growly shiver.

He was shivering a little now, looking down at the snow below. He was wondering how long it might be till he crashed down into it.

"It's wings would have to be wider than any other glider. By about a third," C.J. had told Growly back then, pointing to his papers. "For greater strength and to be more stable in the wind. And it would need a special harness for the … er … *extra weight*."

The *extra weight* was standing in front of him now, looking back with a nervous grin.

"Are you ready Chippy?" Growly asked. "Remember, if we start going down, pull this strap and you'll be released."

"Ok," Gittel said, taking in a long, deep breath. "Remember, run together, keep the nose steady and …" (all three of them said together), "Don't crash into the snow!"

On the count of three, Growly and Chippy took off down the platform, running closely strapped together as they counted out the steps. "Seven … eight … nine … and … GO!"

With a last heaving push, they leapt out into the air. For a moment they felt the glider drop, and then, suddenly it caught the wind and they were lifted upward. Chippy let out a happy shout, and there was a roar of cheering and applause from the enormous crowd that had gathered. There were hundreds of bears on the hillside, and many more out in the meadow just beyond.

Growly felt the glider wobble and jitter in the wind. It felt very different than his own glider, and the weight of Chippy below him took a lot of getting used to. They circled up higher for a moment, Growly tilting and turning as they went, to get a feel for the steering controls.

"It handles well!" Growly shouted to Chippy, loud so that he could be heard above the wind. We better head down now though." He pointed out to one of the wingtips. "Ice! It's already starting to form."

"Ice will be one of your biggest challenges, at least until you get below the clouds," C.J. had told them. "And landing—that's a challenge that could hurt quite a bit."

As Growly swooped down above the meadow now, he called out to Chippy to get ready for the count.

"Three … two … one … and … LIFT!" Growly pulled back hard on the steering bar, lifting the nose of the glider high and bringing them to a sudden, snowy stop. In a moment, there were bears gathered all around, cheering and shouting and helping Growly and Chippy out of their harness.

"How long?" Growly asked, as C.J. came toward them holding his watch.

"A minute and a half," C.J. said, looking worried, "and that's on a sunny day. By the look of the ice already on the wing, much longer and you might have crashed. I've got a few ideas though. Come on, that's enough for today."

They continued to practice throughout the next week, with C.J. trying oils and treatments on the wings. "Three minutes," C.J. said with some satisfaction. "That's twice as much as when we started."

"Three minutes can be enough, if I circle down steeply," Growly said. "It has to be enough."

C.J. knew Growly was right. A scouting team had just returned from across the Great River. The ice near the blocked falls had piled high and wide throughout the winter, and it wouldn't be long until it started to move.

"You can do it in three minutes, Growly. You're right. It is time for you both to leave."

They walked out of Haven the next morning, a long trail of bears that stretched back all the way to the Lookout. They had said their goodbyes the night before, with an enormous, though still rationed, feast all along the main street of Haven.

They would fly down over the open land at the

foot of The Precipice, continuing over the jungles to the a clearing where the monkeys of Towerwood had built landings for their zip lines. From there they would go on foot, with just enough food for their journey, and no other supplies.

"You must be as light as possible!" C.J. had reminded them at the feast. "So, I think I should probably eat that piece of pie for you."

C.J. was waiting for them down at The Precipice now. He had left before sunrise with Gittel and some of the pilots to help prepare the glider and clear any snow from the takeoff path. As they made their way down the Little Cliffs, Ember walked by Growly's side, going over the plans again, and trying not to be worried.

"We are making more progress with the digging now," she said. "It's still very slow with all the ice, but I think in a few weeks it will get easier. We have a very big team of engineers, now that we also have the ones from Arborstone. As soon as you warn Towerwood and get them to safety we should be ready to meet you. Oh, Growly! Be careful!"

"We will be careful, Ember," Growly said seriously. "There are a lot of monkeys who need us to be, and I want to come home as soon as I possibly can to … to see you."

"You father and his team will get the Cascade

diverted, Growly," Ember said. "And once Annily and I get back, we will make our way down to come and meet you. Oh Growly, I can't wait to visit Towerwood."

"When will he leave?" Growly asked. He had hardly had a chance to talk to Ember over the last few days, and C.J. had been so busy with the glider he'd had little time for other things.

"In two days," Ember said, "Balliwick and some of the others from Arborstone will be going back across the Great River for supplies. He said that he would look in the place they've stored some books. For something that has copies of the writings."

"Do you think there might be a clue to where you came from Ember?" Growly could see the hope in her eyes as he said it. He paused, and then smiled before he continued. "Balliwick said the cave is filled writings. If there's anywhere that might hold a clue, that's the place to start looking."

He thought back to the words Balliwick had written on the paper. One part of a sentence, written in the language of people. "...*long have we been looking, in search of those we lost long ago...*" C.J. and Merridy had already been studying Heflin's writings in the cave on Heflin's Reach.

"Every clue points northward," Merridy had told him.

"That's where Heflin headed, and that's where he hoped others were too," said Ember. "The People writings could be the answer to it all. With Mama and

… Papa's help …" Ember paused and took a deep breath. It still almost made her cry to think she had a father now. "With their help, Growly …maybe we really can find where I am from."

"I'll miss you, Ember," Growly said. " Make sure you and Annily keep C.J. and Merridy on track. You know how silly those two can be when they are together!"

Ember laughed and gave Growly a hug. "Yes Growly, I do. They're wonderful."

They reached The Precipice as the late morning sun spread out over the Lower Lands. C.J. and his team had the glider ready, its wide wings stretched out in the warm sunlight, facing a path of open ground that led to the edge of the cliff.

"The conditions are wonderful," Gittel was saying, as she strapped Growly and Chippy into their harness. "Low winds and no chance of snow. Now fly carefully, you two."

With their harnesses checked, Growly and Chippy stood facing The Precipice. The weight of the glider was supported by bears on either side who were helping steady the wings.

"Are you ready?" Growly asked Chippy. His voice sounded shaky and full of fear.

Chippy didn't answer, but just nodded once, looking back at Growly as his body gently shivered.

"Ok ... five ... four ... three ..." They were running down the path, their boots thumping on the frozen ground as they came closer to the edge. "Two ... one ..." And then they were suddenly out in the air, over the edge of The Precipice.

24
Clouds

rowly felt the glider drop for a few heart pounding moments before the updraft caught it and they lifted out over the drop. There was a cheer from the crowd watching back on the cliff edge and shouts of encouragement that were muffled by the wind.

Chippy gritted his teeth tight. He knew what was about to happen next.

"Hold on tight, Chippy!" Growly shouted. "The downdraft will hit us in a ..."

Suddenly the glider was pushed downward, as Growly fought to keep control.

"Don't fight against it too much," C.J. had told him. "Though you would know this as well as I do. Circle steadily downward. You're not going to crash into the ground any time soon."

Growly put the glider into a wide, downward spiral, trying to descend as quickly as possible before ice began to form on the wings.

"Once you get a little lower, you'll have clear winds

for a short while, that is until you reach the clouds. It's always rough in the clouds," C.J. had said with a weak smile. "At least that's how it was for me, and for you too, Growly."

Growly pushed the nose of the glider downward. He had been counting as they circled, trying to keep track of how long it had been since they leapt off the cliff. Three minutes? Or was it two?

As if hearing his thoughts, Chippy shouted above the wind. "Three and a half minutes! Growly, look!

Chippy was pointing out to the tip of the right wing, where tiny glittering crystals of ice were beginning to form.

Growly felt his heart pounding. They were still a long way above the clouds. "I'm going to put it into a steep dive, Chippy. Hold on!"

There was no need for those instructions. Chippy's hands were locked to the grip bar in front of him, his knuckles white and aching under his gloves.

Growly pushed the nose of the glider downward as steeply as he dared, sending them suddenly into a plummeting dive. The wind, which had been whistling by and flapping in the glider wings, now howled around them, and the glider shook as it shot downward. Growly glanced out at the wings. The ice was growing by the second, spreading out along the edge of the wings.

"The clouds!" Chippy shouted, tearing one of his gloved hands away from the grip bar to point to what lay just ahead.

"Ok," Growly thought to himself, counting in his mind, "three ... two ... and..."

As he sped downward he suddenly heaved back on the steering bar, sending them whooshing along the top of the clouds. It was a wonderful feeling to be suddenly out of the dive, and Chippy let out a happy shout, reaching down just below him to see what a cloud might feel like.

They were just there for a moment though. As they steadied from the dive, Growly pushed the nose forward again, sending them down into the dim, swirling blanket of fog.

"Hold on!" Growly cried again, as the glider was

twisted and tossed. He and Chippy had talked about this part of the flight and how rough it would be.

"Once you get into the clouds the winds will be warmer, so you won't have to worry so much about ice," C.J. had said. "Just concentrate on staying steady. At least as steady as you can."

The glider bumped and jostled about, sometimes dropping suddenly and other times lifting up again, pushed wildly on an upward wind. Other than the occasional flashes of piercing sunlight, there was no way to see very far through the thick, swirling gloom.

"Before you reach the clouds, make sure you are heading away from the cliffs." That's what C.J. had told him. "And when you're in the clouds, keep your glider as straight as you can. Better to fly too far out to the south, than to turn and risk flying …"

"… into The Precipice!" Growly had finished the sentence, and they had both felt a shiver.

Growly pushed the nose of the glider forward again. As they raced on, he peered ahead through the dimness, looking for any sign of light up ahead. How long had they been going? He had completely lost track of time.

All of a sudden an updraft sent them twisting to the right, lifting and turning them as Growly fought for control. "Chippy!" Growly cried. "Keep your eye on the compass! We have to keep heading south!"

Chippy was just about to answer back when the glider suddenly began to fall, caught now on a downdraft that spun them sharply once again. The monkey felt his sight going blurry and dizziness making everything spin.

"Chippy! The compass!" He could hear Growly's voice from somewhere far away. Somewhere past the howling wind and the world which seemed to continue to spin and spin and spin.

"Chippington!" Growly's voice sounded very far away now. Chippy was desperately trying to stay conscious. Chippington? Growly hardly ever called him that. Chippy was doing the best he could to fight the dizziness, to remember where he was.

"Chippington! The compass!"

The compass! Glider! … Chippy pushed past the dizziness, fighting to open his eyes and focus on the grip bar in front of him. There was a small compass attached in the middle, with a wildly swinging needle.

"Left, Growly!" Chippy shouted. Doing all he could to focus on the needle. "That way is south."

Growly swung the glider to the left, making a sharp, plummeting turn as he dove back downward.

"Now keep it straight!" Growly whispered to himself. His arms were aching and his paws felt like they were locked to the steering bar. The air here was warmer though; it felt like it was beginning to thaw the icy feeling in his cheeks.

The glider whistled and rattled as it shot downward through the clouds, the canvas of the wings flapping and humming.

Light! Somewhere down below Growly thought he had seen a flash of green. "Did you see it?" he cried.

Chippy looked up for a moment with a puzzled expression on his face and shook his head.

"See what, Gr …?"

"Look!" Growly cried, and Chippy spun back around, peering down into the clouds in the direction Growly was pointing.

"Ground!" Chippy cried happily. "Ground! Ground!"

Growly heaved on the steering bar, bringing the nose of the glider upward as they shot out of the clouds. Far below them stretched the rolling hills and meadows on the edge of the Upper Jungle. The hills were green and covered in wildflowers. It never snowed this close to the jungles.

"Just a few more miles!" Chippy shouted happily. "It was his homeland, and he was soon to be touching it with his feet! "Growly! We made it."

Growly grinned. "Almost. Just one more thing."

Pulling hard on the steering bar, Growly turned the glider in a wide, sweeping turn to the left, sending them out and around a tall range of hills. From here they could follow the ridge for a little while, cutting out over the jungle farther to the north. As they were about to turn in that direction, Chippy pointed out to the left. "Look Growly! There. The Alps!"

Growly could see the tall, snow covered mountains far in the distance, some of the peaks disappearing into thick, black clouds. It gave him a strange, unsettled feeling that he couldn't quite understand.

He pulled on the bar again, swinging the glider to

the right. Turning hard, they came around the hills, gaining some height before swooping out across the meadows which were already lush and green.

The meadows raced by underneath them until suddenly they came to the edge of the trees and they were soaring above the twisting, tangled jungle. Growly remembered the last time he was here in a glider, and he felt a little shiver, lifting the nose of the glider upward to stay high above the trees.

It was impossible to see the ground through the thick canopy of the treetops. Everything was just leafy green for as far as he could see in front of him. It would be easy to lose direction if it wasn't for Chippy.

The monkey watched eagerly as they covered the miles, smiling happily as they raced over his homeland below. They had been flying for a long time when suddenly Chippy shouted excitedly, tugging on Growly's jacket in case he hadn't heard.

"The zip lines, Growly! Just up ahead." Growly had almost missed it at first, as the horizon was hidden in misty haze. Just up ahead though, he saw the ridge line, a place he had visited a long time ago. At least it felt like a long time ago. So much had happened, and so many miles had been crossed, all with his friend who was dangling beneath him.

They whooshed out over the edge of the ridge, and suddenly the ground dropped away, falling steeply down towering cliffs to more jungle below. There were the zip lines down at the base of the cliffs, stretching out over the treetops to towers far in the distance.

Growly put the glider into a wide turn, heading steadily downward toward the towers and a grassy clearing just beyond.

"There!" Chippy called, pointing to a wide, flat place, not far from the first trees at the edge of the jungle.

As they came close to the ground, Growly pulled back hard on the steering handle, lifting the nose of the glider and bringing it to a (mostly) sudden stop. As they touched the ground, Chippy yanked the release strap excitedly, rolling to the grass with a happy shout. "The ground! *My* ground! Growly! Look. Grass!!"

Growly let out a happy laugh, falling to the soft grass and stretching his arms and legs out wide. It felt soft and solid and wonderful all at once. He took in a deep breath of the fresh meadow breeze, and then stopped, sitting up suddenly. Smoke! Not strong, but sure in the wind.

Chippy smelled it too, and he sat up with a puzzled look on his face. "Jungle fire?" he said, gazing out into the trees.

"I think we need to go and find out," Growly said urgently. "It could be close to Towerwood."

25
On the Beaten Path

With their glider quickly stowed, the two friends ran toward the trees, following a trampled path that went onward into the thick undergrowth of vines and bushes beneath the jungle canopy. As they came to the trees, Chippy slowed to a walk, with puzzled concern spreading over his face.

"Look Growly," he said slowly, pointing around him at the trampled bushes and broken branches along the path ahead of them.

Growly had noticed it too. Though he didn't know a lot about jungles, he knew a lot about forests and how to read the signs of a large group coming through.

"Many!" Chippy said with a gasp. "Many many! Hundreds!"

"But who?" Growly asked, his eyes wide as they pushed deeper in under the trees. "They are going *toward* Towerwood."

"Come on Growly!" Chippy said. He was already

beginning to run. "Something's wrong! We have to hurry!" He shouted the last few words from farther down the path, stopping and waving to Growly before he took off again.

Growly was running now too, following the monkey as his mind tried to make sense of it all. He could still smell the smoke in the air, sour and sharp. Not like a fire at home. It reminded him of something. Something he *couldn't quite put his paw on* (as the saying went).

He caught up to Chippy quickly, and the two of them ran together as the hours passed, stopping only to drink at the streams for a moment before continuing on their way. All around them were the signs of a large group, traveling quickly by the look of things.

"Boot prints!" Chippy gasped, as they came to a wide, muddy slope in the late afternoon. They were getting close to Towerwood now ... just a few more miles.

Growly knelt down next to Chippy, examining the churned up, slippery ground. It *was* boot prints. That was certain. Many of them. The slope was filled with the signs of boots and shoes and the slips and stumbles of a very large group.

"Bears?" Chippy asked, looking up at Growly with a puzzled look on his face. "Too big for monkeys ... except these small bootprints."

Growly slowly shrugged. "It ... it could be ... but from where?"

Chippy was thoughtful for a moment, looking back down at the footprints in the mud. "Little ones!" he whispered." Lots of little ones. Look Growly! So many Cubs!"

It was true. Growly could see many of the footprints were small, at least further up the slope where the ground was drier. As if they had been carried across the mud.

"Up there!" Chippy gasped, pointing into the bushes ahead of them. A moment later, Growly saw it too, something that looked like matted fur, with a bright strip of red cloth wrapped around it, almost hidden under some leaves.

Slogging through the thick mud, they slipped and slid up the steep slope, coming eventually to firmer ground and the strange, furry shape under the leaves. Chippy dropped to his knees, lifting up the little object for Growly to see.

"A bear!" Chippy said slowly, his eyes wide with wonder.

It *was* a bear. Growly could see it right away. A toy bear dressed in a red shirt, with bright green shorts and spattered with mud.

Growly and Chippy stared at each other in astonishment. It was a well loved toy. Growly could see where it had been patched and re-patched in places. For it to be left behind here in the jungle …

"We have to hurry!" Growly said suddenly, leaping to his feet. "Something *is* very wrong. I've been feeling it more and more all day. Now this toy bear and the smoke. Chippy, it reminds me of ..."

"Rivers of fire!" Chippy finished the sentence before Growly could get the words out. "I was thinking it, Growly. I didn't want to say."

The rivers of fire had been frightening for both of them, back when they were searching for C.J. But Chippy had to face the fires the most, and it still scared the young monkey so much that he could hardly bear to think about it. When he had recognized the smell, earlier in the day, it had filled him with alarm. He had hoped that perhaps it was just his imagination.

"Towerwood!" Growly exclaimed, taking off up the hill.

Chippy took a deep breath. If there were rivers of fire nearby, his hometown had to be warned.

They rushed along the path, slipping and sliding now as they hurried onward along the path. They had come to an area Growly recognized now, with tall, rocky outcrops and gigantic boulders in amongst the trees. Just a little bit further and ... yes... there it was: a narrow pass in between two large rocks.

They came out onto a high cliff, overlooking a sparkling blue lake far, far below. And there, out in the middle of the lake, on a wide island with a thick forest of trees. Towerwood.

The scene before them was completely unexpected. The smoke of hundreds of campfires twisted up into the air over the island. The beaches and grassy slopes, once home to wild flowers and sprawling gardens, were now packed with a city of tents and shelters. Tiny figures hurried about between the tents, but it was too far away from the cliffs though to see who, or what, they might be.

Towerwood itself was busy too. The lights from the houses sparkled brightly up into the branches of the enormous hardwoods at the center of the village.

Growly could see that Chippy was upset. For so long he had been talking about what it would be like to see his home again. And now, to see it like this. Growly could tell Chippy's mind was racing, putting pieces together and thinking what to do next. He had seen that look on his friend's face many times before.

"The zip lines, Growly," he said suddenly, hurrying along the ledge to a platform which Growly remembered well. He had been on zip lines twice before. One time it was wonderful. The other time, well…

"They're gone!" Chippy cried in alarm. "There is always at least one handle here! Why …" He didn't finish his sentence, already trying to think of what to do next.

"Come on!" he said after a moment, waving for Growly to follow as he began to run off again into the trees.

They made their way for a while on a path that followed the edge of the cliff, twisting in and out of the jungle until they came to a tall, jagged, pile of rocks. There was a wide door here, built in amongst the boulders, the stonework worn and weathered with age. The door itself was newer than the stone, though by its color and smoothness, Growly could see it was very, very old.

"Cave," Chippy said, as he pulled on the polished brass handle and swung the heavy door wide, "to the docks."

Going inside, Chippy took an unlit lantern from a shelf on the wall. There was a flint with it too, and soon bright light lit the inky blackness of the tunnel. It was a stairway, Growly could see, twisting steeply down toward a dim glow far, far below. They climbed downward for a long time, step after step. Finally, they came out into a wide, bright room, filled with dazzling sunlight from a large window overlooking the lake. The roof shimmered and sparkled from the sunshine reflecting off the waves, making Growly feel like he was deep underwater.

"It's beautiful, Chippy!" Growly whispered in wonder. The whole room seemed to quiver and dance with light.

Chippy nodded. "It was here before monkeys," he said softly and reverently. "Remiki found it when he discovered the island. *The Cave of Colors*. It changes through the day."

They hurried across the room, finally reaching another large door on the other side. "The Docks," Chippy said, stepping out into the daylight, "and Bo ..." He was meaning to say "Boats." But as he stepped through the door, his eyes went wide again in confusion and surprise. "Wha ...?'

There were three large docks, strewn with ropes and large sacks and part of a sail. But not a single boat could be seen anywhere.

"Always boats, Growly! There are always boats here." The young monkey took off again, turning back toward the doorway and racing back into the cave.

"The other docks, Growly! Come on!"

Growly hurried after him, running through the Cave of Colors to another large doorway on the far side.

Chippy was already turning the handle, looking back at Growly as he heaved with all his might.

The door swung wide and a rush of afternoon breeze swept into the room, along with a blinding dazzle of afternoon light.

"Chippington!?" A shocked monkey voice came from somewhere just outside the door.

"Growly!?" Another voice, which made Growly jump back in complete, absolute astonishment.

26

Old Friends & How to Help

ourtland!" Growly gasped. He could not make out the face of the figure outside in the dazzling sunlight, but there was no mistaking that voice. It wasn't a bear voice or a monkey voice either. It was a *people* voice. Courtland, from the village of West Evony, the man by the sea. But what was he doing here?

Growly stumbled out into the sunlight, putting his paw up to shield his eyes so they could adjust to the brightness.

"Growly!" Courtland said it again, his voice filled with wonder as he stepped forward and threw his arms around the very confused bear. "We ... we never knew when we might see you again. When Meegwin told us of the way up The Precipice, of it being blocked again, and the broken gates we found washed over ... and ... Chippington!?"

Courtland tuned to Chippy, who at that moment was being surrounded by a crowd of bewildered monkey friends. Meegwin was there. The elder

monkey stood in between Growly and Chippy, his eyes
wide as he looked from one to the other, as if they had
just appeared right out of thin air. Barbod and
Tappen were there as well—two of Chippy's friends
who had rescued Growly from the lake on his first
visit to Towerwood. They all stood in silent
amazement for a moment longer, and then, as if
someone had given a signal, everyone was talking at
once, shouting and cheering in surprise, blurting out
"how?" and "when?" between the laughter and the
hugs.

It was Meegwin who finally got everyone to calm
down a little, urging all the monkeys to stand back and
to hush for a moment so Chippy could speak. Growly
could tell the librarian was bursting with as much
excitement as the monkeys gathered around.

"Meegwin!" Chippy gasped at last. "Friends …"
The young monkey paused for a moment as he saw
that that dock was filled with others. *People!* Chippy
blinked, and tried not to let his mouth drop open in
shock.

"Um … *everyone?*" he stammered. Chippy looked
over at Meegwin, his expression full of questions.

Meegwin smiled encouragingly. "It's a long story,
Chippington. A lot has happened since you've been
away. We are just on our way back to West Evony.
There is much danger near the people's village."

The word hit Chippy with a jolt.

"Danger!" Chippy gasped, remembering the
mountains of ice and piling water high up on The

Precipice. They had come to warn the monkeys of Towerwood of what would surely be coming.

Chippy glanced quickly across the waters of the lake, to the city of tents on the beaches of the island.

"Danger, Meegwin! *Towerwood* is in danger!" Chippy spoke quickly in Monkey, but Growly had learned enough to be able to understand.

"Water is coming—a big flood of water. It could be any day. We have come as quickly as we could, but the water may already be on its way."

Meegwin stared at Chippy for a moment, his mind racing as the young monkey's words began to sink in. Suddenly he turned to Courtland, speaking quickly to the man in Bear. It confused Growly for a moment, but then it all started to make sense. Courtland and Meegwin both knew Bear, but Meegwin didn't know how to speak *People*, and Courtland didn't know Monkey. Bear was the only language they both understood.

"Courtland!" Meegwin exclaimed. "We have to get everyone off the beaches. Into the trees for now if possible. I know most of the tree homes are full, but we will double up again if we have to."

Courtland nodded, though he looked completely confused.

"Chippington says floods are coming. He and Growly came here to try and warn us."

Courtland suddenly turned, waving his hand high and shouting out words that Growly couldn't understand. There were gasps from some of the gathered men and shouts of alarm. Then suddenly everyone was moving. Men and monkeys raced back along the dock, heading toward two large sailboats with sails still flapping gently in the afternoon breeze.

"All aboard!" Barbod called, turning back to make sure all the monkeys were heading to their places. As Chippy rushed by, Barbod clapped him joyfully on the shoulder. Everyone had feared Chippy might never return.

The boats sped out across the lake, cutting through the small, choppy waves with sails full and humming. Chippy and Growly stood with Meegwin and Courtland, the two monkeys deep in urgent discussion, while Growly did his best to translate for the leader of the People village.

"We began working together a long while ago, not long after you went with Growly up The Precipice." Meegwin was saying. "We've had teams there, helping them build boats and learn sailing. They believe there might be a way to find the People land, the one where others just like them come from. But the danger …" Meegwin seemed like he hardly dared to say it. "We were on our way to call back those still working on the boats."

Growly's mind was racing. Danger? What could Meegwin be talking about? He looked closely at Courtland. "Did you see it?" Growly whispered. "What kind of danger is it?"

Courtland was about to answer when there was a shout from the monkeys at the bows of the two boats, and then other shouts from monkeys on the long docks which stretched out from the beaches of Towerwood Island. Crowds of monkeys and people were running out to see why the sailboats were returning so soon, and all along the beaches more were on their way.

As the boats came up alongside the dock, Meegwin and Courtland leaped out into the crowd, calling out in Monkey and People for silence, and for everyone to step back to give those on the boats some room. Courtland had given his men on the boat instructions as they sailed. Now they led those from West Evony back toward the beaches, not saying anything yet about the danger of flooding. They didn't want to cause panic.

Meegwin did the same. All the monkeys waited with him on the docks, the older ones at least. Those with young were asked to go up to the grassy slopes. There was a worried hush over everyone now. Meegwin had given the signal, which every monkey past a certain age understood. When that signal was given, those monkeys had been trained and trained in what to do. When Meegwin gave the news, there weren't even any questions. Those trained for such emergencies would meet at the Town Hall. Everyone else would help get Courtland's people off the beach.

"Bring everyone to the central meeting area," Meegwin was saying "Don't worry about the tents yet! The rescue team and the grownups will get them after the children are up high and safe. Idalia, would you help in finding places in the ..." Meegwin's words trailed off as he saw the tear's streaming down Chippy's mother's face. She hardly dared to believe her eyes.

"Mamma!" Chippy cried. He was pushing his way through the crowd. Reaching his mother, he wrapped his arms around the sobbing monkey.

"I'll ... um ..." Meegwin looked away and took a deep breath before he could continue. "Jacory, could you handle that?"

Jacory nodded respectfully as he leaped from the boat and took off at a run down the dock toward the village.

"Chippington Chippy!" came a delighted cry, as a small monkey pushed her way through the crowd.

"Eka!" Chippy gasped, letting go of his mother for a moment as he knelt down to catch his little sister in his arms.

"Chippington Chippy!" she cried "Chippington Chippy! I knew you would come back! Look how big I am now!"

Chippy grinned through the tears. Chippington Chippy. She had started calling him that when Growly first came to Towerwood.

"You *are* so big!" Chippy laughed with a happy sniff. "You'll be as big as Remiki in no time."

"That big!?" Eka gasped, looking up at Chippy, her eyes wide in wonder. Remiki, the founder of Towerwood, was far bigger than any monkey ever. At least that's what the stories and legends said anyway.

They were all on their way then, with Meegwin in

the lead. As they came to the island, monkeys broke off in different directions, each to their assigned tasks. Many of the group would stay to help those on the beaches, and to make sure that none of the younger monkeys were left behind.

To the trees. That's where the mothers and their children were headed. To the homes and bridges, offices and stores nestled high in the branches of Towerwood. Many people were already staying with monkey families, but now every high space would be used. The flooding could come at any time. They would make a plan of escape soon, but right now everyone needed to move to safety.

"Growly, Chippington, we must go to the town hall," Meegwin said. "The rescue team will already be assembling, along with the mayor and the Council of Elders. Courtland, we will need you also. We have to act quickly, it seems, on behalf of monkeys and people … and a bear." He added, looking at Growly with a sudden gentleness, and throwing his arm around the Young Bear's shoulder in a strong and heartfelt hug.

27

What Kind of Danger?

hippy stared out at the scene below him from the long, polished wooden bridge, which led up from the Town Hall into the forest where the village of Towerwood was built amongst the branches. How many times had he played on this bridge when he was little? He smiled at a memory of Tappen swinging from a rope he had tied there, unable to climb back up and unable to drop to the ground. He had to be rescued. It was Chippy's father, Badru, who had gotten him down. That was back in the days when C.J. lived here. Those days felt like a lifetime ago.

It had always been a peaceful place, Towerwood, with the sounds of the lake and the gentle afternoon breezes whispering through the trees. Even the squeals of little monkeys seemed peaceful in this place. It was not that way now though. Down below, monkeys and people ran this way and that, carrying boxes and bundles up into the heights. Boats were already arriving at the main dock, to carry mothers and the youngest ones to the Cave of Colors. A campsite would be made in the jungle to the east, in a clearing just beyond the top of the cliffs.

"Everyone has to leave?"

A sad, small voice shook Chippy from his thoughts. Eka. He looked down at his little sister with a gentle smile, trying to look as brave and encouraging as he could.

"Every single monkey. Even Meegwin! Can you believe it, Eka? You are a part of history!"

Eka smiled, though it was a smile which was very unsure and very shaky.

Chippy knelt down and gave her a hug. That was exactly how he felt too—very unsure and very shaky.

"It's a good thing monkeys live in trees," Eka said after a moment, looking up at the twinkling lights in the forest. "Remiki was smart when he thought of that, but …" All of a sudden a thought came into her mind and she let out a worried gasp, "… but … the *LIBRARY!* What about all the books!?"

Chippy nodded. There were many buildings on the ground amongst the forest. Stores and offices, workshops and bakeries. But the library was the biggest of them all, taking up two floors under the Village House. There were many treasures in the village of Towerwood, but not much of more value than the collection of books.

"Every monkey will carry one when they leave, Eka. Meegwin is selecting the order now. There are caves on the cliffs where they can be safely stored. The ones that can't be carried, we'll store high up in the trees."

Eka smiled, a little more confidently now.

"Mama will be here in a moment, and then I'll have to go," Chippy said softly, "but I'll see you later at the campsite. Can you be brave until then?"

"I will, Chippington Chippy," Eka said with an earnest nod. "I'll draw lots of pictures for you to see when you come."

Growly wiped his forehead and took a deep breath. The weather here was always warm, even in the final days of winter. For the last few hours he had been working with Courtland, bundling tents and supplies on the beach with the people of West Evony.

The meeting at the Village House had been short and serious. Chippy told of what they had seen at the top of The Precipice—enormous chunks of ice, far, far more than the bears of Arborstone had ever seen. And the flooding of Arborstone village! More water up in the Salington Sea than had ever been before, at least since the days of Hegel. Towerwood Lake always rose higher in the spring, but this was different.

A plan had quickly been formed. Boats would begin to take the youngest ones across the lake to the caverns, where they would climb to higher ground. Those who stayed would move as much as they could up into the homes and buildings, high in the trees. It could be days, or even weeks till the waters came, and much could be saved in that time. A team of monkeys would journey up the river to The Precipice, traveling along the lower cliffs to stay safe from any flooding. They would light a signal fire, warning the others when the waters finally came.

"Four hours!" the mayor had said seriously. "Maybe five at the most. That's how long we'll have from the time we see the signal till the floodwaters reach Towerwood."

"That's the last of the tents," Courtland panted, walking over to Growly and crouching down to catch his breath. "I wish we could be more help to the monkeys, but there was only a small group of men who came with the mothers and children of West Evony. Most of the men are still far in the south, in the cove by the Ocean."

"C.J.'s Cove?!" Growly asked. He had been so busy he hadn't even had time to think to ask Courtland about "the danger" and why the people of his village were here.

Courtland smiled. "Yes, C.J.'s Cove, though it has another name. *Aralyn's Firth*. Named after the wife of Crevan. I think you know about him."

Growly blinked in surprise. Crevan. One of the ancient explorers who had found a way up The Precipice. He had built a large castle in the Alps that divided these jungles from the Ocean. C.J. had wondered if the buildings in the Cove may have been built by him and his people too.

"I went to Morningfeld, Growly," Courtland continued, "with my wife and a small team of historians from our village. We found writings about the cove, and of abandoned cities in the islands, and Growly," Courtland leaned closer with excitement, holding tightly to Growly's arm, "perhaps a way to find their home! The land of *people*, Growly! The place where *we* came from!"

Growly remembered the story Courtland had told him long ago, about the people of his village of West Evony. Their ancestors had been shipwrecked over 400 years ago. Many of those had been children, and over the years much of their history had been lost and forgotten. No one in West Evony knew from where that ancient ship had come.

"The men of the West Evony are building boats, with the help of some of the monkeys of this village. With these large boats, we will sail to the Endless Islands. That will be the first part of our voyage. We were getting close to completion when ... well ... when we saw the danger. We knew we had to get everyone who was not working to safety."

"The *danger*?" Growly whispered. "What *kind* of danger is it?"

Courtland looked at Growly even more closely, lowering his voice as if he thought Growly wasn't going to believe what he said next.

"*Fire,* Growly! The Alps are on fire!"

Growly let out a loud gasp, which almost sounded like a cry.

"*Rivers* of fire?" he said in a quivering voice. He could feel a sick feeling rising up in his stomach.

Courtland stepped back in surprise.

"You've seen them?!" he whispered. "Many of the mountains are burning now. At least that's how it looks."

"The horses!" Growly cried suddenly. "Oh Courtland, I have to go find Chippy!"

Growly took off along the beach, stumbling over the pebbly ground, up onto the grassy banks, and then off through the banana bushes toward the boathouses at the far end of the island. Chippy was helping a team ready more boats, especially the larger ones he had been working on before he went to find C.J.

As he burst through the door of the main workshop, Growly searched for his friend amongst the bustle of activity. An enormous boat filled most of the space, stretching out onto the lake through the open wall near the front. As Growly came further into the room, Chippy's head appeared over the railing of the boat.

"Growly?" Chippy could see at once that Growly was upset. "Growly. What is it?"

"Morningfeld!" Growly gasped, trying to catch his breath. "The smoke we smelled. Fire!" Growly stopped for a moment and took a deep breath. "Chippy, we have help the horses!"

28
Water

Growly awoke from his dreams with a start, sitting up in his bed and looking around in confusion. He had been dreaming of Haven, or more specifically, of Ember. She was walking into the woods, just a little way ahead of him. Calling out his name as if she didn't know where he was. "I'm back here!" he had called. "Right behind you. Over here!" And in his dream she would stop still at times and listen, as if she almost heard his voice.

He remembered so many dreams like this. Oh, how he missed her. They were Young Bears now. It was the time when they should be preparing for the future, for family, and for their hopes and dreams ahead.

"Two years a Young Bear,
and then you are grown,
Two years to form plans,
and to build yee a home.
(Growly loved the "yee" part.)

Two years a Young Bear,
Then a grown bear yee be,
With a hat on yee head
And a Cub on yee knee.

"Two Years a Young Bear" was a very old poem, which had been around since the days of Hegel. That's probably where all the "yees" came from, though most bears thought the writer had just added them for fun. It didn't have to be two years, of course. For some bears it was three years, or two and a half. But at some point there was the ceremony, *The Passing of the Hat,* where a father would give his ceremonial hat to his son, or a mother to her daughter. And just like that, a Young Bear would be a … well … just a Bear. There was no special name for it until you became an Elder. No one knew why. "Grown-Up Bear" just didn't seem to fit.

Growly sighed. He already had a home. And one day he and Ember would … he shook his head sadly. Home felt so far away right now.

They had been in Towerwood for more than a week now, storing the heavy furniture in the highest buildings and taking belongings across the lake in the boats. There was still no sign from the monkeys by The Precipice, though the water was rising every day. The beach was fully underwater now, and the lake came halfway up the grassy slopes.

Most of the monkeys were living in the camp clearing above the cliffs, along with the people of West

Evony. Monkeys knew how to forage and find fruit and nuts in the jungle, and their joyful songs and encouraging smiles lifted the hearts of the little children, and the grownups too.

Growly was desperate to be going. Every day he worried about the fires in the Alps and the horses who called that place their home.

It was Chippy though who seemed even more anxious. "They're trapped Growly," he would whisper. "I promised I would help them!"

They could not go yet though. Every monkey (and bear) who could help was needed in Towerwood. There was still much to do before the floodwaters arrived.

Growly slid out of his bed and walked softly across the floor, dressing quickly in his outside clothes and his worn and dusty hiking boots.

Suddenly, there was a loud banging on the door, followed be Chippy's anxious call. "Growly! *Growly!* The signal! It's coming!"

Growly felt his heart leap and pound as he fumbled with the door handle. The water!

Flinging the door wide, Growly stepped out into the cool, early morning light. Monkeys were running on the ground far below, and the sound of a bell now tolled above the Village House.

"Four hours?" Growly gasped, thinking quickly through all they had to do.

"No!" Chippy's face looked ashen. "There was big fog in the night. We just saw the signal now! It might be much less!"

Chippy was talking fast and his eyes were wide. They had known this could be a danger. That the signal might be hidden. But now that it was happening …

"We know what we have to do, Chippy," Growly said, as calmly as he could. "We have to search all the buildings. To make sure everybody knows. Then we get to the docks, as quickly as we can."

Chippy nodded, the frantic look on his face beginning to calm a little. "We search together. Two by two. Remember? Starting at the Boat House and back through the village." Chippy's voice grew more sure as he said it.

"Your backpack, Growly. Now we run."

They met Barbod on the long, winding path that led to the Boat House. He was dressed in his hiking clothes, with his strange, round cap pulled tightly just above his ears. His sailor's cap—that's what everyone called it. No one loved the lake more than Barbod, and no one sailed anywhere near as well as he did.

Barbod was usually very quiet. He seldom smiled (or frowned for that matter), but would listen with his head and shoulders tall and straight. When he spoke, his words were usually slow and stumbling. If you didn't know him, you might think—well, you probably wouldn't know what to think. He constantly looked as if the world around him was a mysterious puzzle.

Chippy understood him though. They had been best friends since before they could walk. Barbod was very, *very* smart and very, *very* funny. Right now though, he looked alarmed. Chippy had never seen him like that.

"The ... the water," he stammered. The sound of alarm bells and horns filled the air now, and there were cries and shouts far off in the distance.

"You know what to do, friend," Chippy said with a soft, confident voice. "Come on, let's go find Tappen."

Barbod barely had time to agree before they were off again down the path, coming at last to the large Boat House built over the water.

"It's ready!" came a shout as they emerged from the trees. It was Tappen, Chippy's *other* best friend from before the time they could walk. Tappen was as different from Barbod as a pineapple to a banana, though they both were very smart and both very funny. Tappen always had a wide grin spread across his face, and he loved to make speeches (to the dismay of his teachers). If Tappen answered a question, it was usually with a preface and then three or four points that explained his position. This was followed by a few alternate views others might have, followed by a list of quotes that may (or may not) be relevant. This could go on and on as long as it was allowed. He didn't try to be rude; everyone knew that. The monkeys of Towerwood often said, "He's just being Tappen! And Tappen has a *lot* of words."

In emergencies, he didn't let his words get in the way. He was a very good sailor and part of the rescue team. No one in Towerwood could run faster or longer than he.

"I've got the last of the ropes on!" Tappen said. "Barbod, the work crew is onboard and the *Jacoby* is rigged and ready to sail."

Growly smiled. Meegwin had told him that Chippy had named the large sailboat in honor of C.J.

Chippy smiled too, but his voice was urgent and serious. "Bring it to the docks and load up. A large crowd is there already. Don't wait for us; you need to go now. We're making a last search through the village. Then we will follow on one of the smaller boats."

Growly and Chippy raced back up the path. As they reached the village, they ran from store to store and from office to office, making sure no one was left behind.

"All clear!" Chippy cried as they came out of the Village House. It had been so strange and unsettling to see the rooms empty and bare and the library with no books.

"Now to the upper levels," Growly gasped. "We just have these three trees."

They bound up a twisting staircase, spiraling its way around the trunk of an enormous hardwood.

They climbed upward and upward until they reached a web of wide bridges and walkways leading higher and higher. On they went, going from house to house and then on to the next.

"Jacory!" Chippy cried as they came into a large home, way up in the highest of the branches. There was a gasp of surprise, and the loud thump of a monkey falling out of bed and onto the floor. "Wha … huh … Chippy … ton?"

Jacory was still half asleep, doing his best to make sense of why he was on the floor. Jacory was the *third* of Chippy's best friends from before they could walk. He could make anything out of anything, and he could *sleep* through anything too.

"Jacory! The water!" Chippy cried. "Right now. We have to go!"

Jacory was still in the work clothes he had been wearing most of the week. He had been working with the engineers, preparing for the flooding and strengthening the walkways most of the night. He definitely was awake *now* though.

With all the buildings checked, they raced down the spiraling stairway, not slowing as they sped across bridges and more stairways to the ground.

"Hurry!" came a cry. It was Chippy's father, Badru, who had run back from the docks to try to find them.

"It's coming! It's coming! The second signal fire. The water is almost here!"

The second signal fire! It *was* almost here. Chippy felt panic swirling up inside. They raced out of the forest and down onto the dock toward a small sailing boat near the end of the pier. It was ready to go, and as they leapt on board, Chippy hauled the sail rope tight, sending the boat out into the waves. The Jacoby was almost to the other side of the lake. Chippy could see its taught sails straining as they pulled toward the far docks.

"Look!" Jacory cried, pointing out across the lake at the river and jungle to the north. Trees were shaking and falling, as a thundering, roaring sound grew louder by the second. The little boat raced across the water. It was one of the fastest in Towerwood, and Chippy had designed it himself.

"Come on," Badru groaned as he glanced again toward the jungle. He was at the rudder, steering as hard as possible toward the docks.

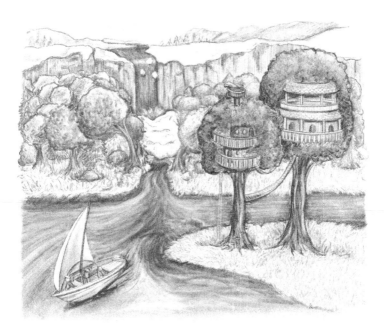

Suddenly an enormous wall of water and broken trees burst out of the distant forest, surging out into the lake, tall and thundering. And behind it, more and more water, as far as could be seen back into the trees. It roared out over the lake, rising higher and higher as it neared the island.

"Brace yourselves!" Badru shouted. "We have to go in fast. As soon as we reach the dock … RUN!"

The little boat hurtled toward the cliffs, and at the last moment, Chippy's father swung the rudder to the right, sending it scraping and screeching along the pier. "Jump!" he cried. "Don't wait for it to stop!"

They leapt from the boat, rolling and tumbling with Badru coming last. Stumbling to their feet they raced toward the caverns, the sound of the thundering floodwaters loud in their ears. Barbod, Tappen, and many of the other monkeys from the Jacoby were waiting at the entrance to the caves, shouting, "Run! Run!" and, "Hurry! Hurry!"

No one had the slightest desire to slow down. They burst into the cave, and soon everyone was racing for the stairway. All of a sudden the surging, raging waters crashed up into the caves.

"Towerwood!" Chippy cried, his voice full of dismay. There was no way back there now.

29

Something Like Hope

They stood silently in the Sad Place, like they did every afternoon. They had made a pact together, to come and watch for an hour, before it was time to go back to the caves and the meadows of Morningfeld. Day after day they had come, week after week, and then month after month. How long had it been? They had almost lost track. The fall had come, and the long, biting winter. Now the signs of first spring were all around, but there was still no sign of the reason they came here.

Everything was different now. Almost everyone had gone to the south, as far away from the smoke and the fire as they could. But even down there the mountains smoldered, and no matter where you went the air was sour and heavy.

"We will leave soon," Flurry said softly. His voice sounded sad and distant, like it was carrying away his last little pieces of hope.

Whisper nudged her little brother gently with her muzzle, neighing softly before she spoke. "Yes, we will.

But we still have some days before we leave. Mama wants us to stay as long as we can after Papa gets back from the south. She thinks there is still a chance."

Flurry looked up at his sister. His eyes were teary, partly from her encouraging voice, and partly from the thick smoke which hung above the cliff. *The cliff!*

Flurry gasped, shaking his mane as he blinked and stepped back in surprise. Up on the cliff! For a moment he thought he had seen a shadow or two!

"Whisper!" he cried. "Whisper! Look!"

Far up on the cliff, surrounded in smoke and haze, were two tiny figures. A tall one with a pack and a smaller one by his side.

"It's them," Whisper cried, leaping joyfully in the air and then turning in a circle. "It *is* them Flurry and, *OH MY!*"

Up on the cliff more figures were appearing, more and more—hundreds of them. Most of them were smaller, but some were even taller than the first two. They looked like the pictures on the walls of the buildings of Morningfeld!

"People!" Flurry gasped. "They *did* come back!"

Whisper felt her heart leap. People had come many months ago, for the first time since the days of Crevan. For the horses of Morningfeld it had been almost unbelievable. Wonderfully unbelievable, and then, heartbreaking. The people had seemed afraid of them, running away whenever the horses came near. And then they had left again, up the cliffs of the Sad Place, just like everyone else had done before.

They were coming back now though! Ropes were dropped from the top of the cliff, bags were lowered, and figures were beginning to make their way downward. Whisper and Flurry ran in happy circles at the foot of the cliff, neighing and whinnying joyfully as those on the ropes got closer.

"It *is* them!" Furry cried as he recognized the shapes of Growly and Chippy. "The ones we carried! Our friends! Our *FRIENDS!*"

Growly could hear the sounds of the horses below him, and, looking downward, he let out a joyful shout to Chippy, nodding toward the meadow.

"The horses!" he cried in delight. "*Our* horses."

Swinging on the rope, Chippy leaped into the air, landing skillfully on a lower ledge before jumping out again. This time he dropped all the way down, tumbling in a drift of snow and bouncing up to throw his arms around Flurry's neck.

After a moment, Chippy swung up onto the young horse's back, while both Flurry and Whisper let out whinnies of delight. Flurry shook his mane happily and took off at a gallop, with Chippy clinging tightly to him, howling with laughter.

As Growly reached the ground he ran over to Whisper. He remembered her deep, dark brown color and the white marking on her head. She had carried him before, and it had been a wonderful feeling, to race through the meadows and along the paths that led through the Alps toward Morningfeld.

"Shall we ride?" Growly asked, dropping his pack

and climbing up onto Whisper's back as she let out another happy whinny in the meadow.

"They've come back!" Whisper thought to herself, her heart almost bursting with joy. And she took off at a run to chase after her brother.

Sawing and chopping sounds filled the air in the forests surrounding the ruins of Morningfeld. Monkeys and men cut beams, and the horses hauled thick, sturdy logs across the fields and pathways, which led back to the Sad Place. It was called the Sad Place because that is where the horses of Crevan's time watched the people of Morningfeld leave them, trapped in the valleys in the midst of the Alps.

"It will need a new name now," Winterfrost said, looking down at her son with an affectionate smile. "Flurry! Look at what they are doing! Can you believe it?"

Flurry looked up at the scurry of activity up on the heights. A wide pathway of scaffolding and bridges was already zig-zagging its way up the side of the cliff, with hundreds of monkeys hammering and cutting as they called out to each other in joyful song. There were people there too, just a few who hadn't gone on to the Cove—Courtland and some of the historians from his village.

Flurry nodded. This place did need a new name now.

"Hope, Mama," he whispered. "It needs a name that means something like that."

It had been three weeks now since Growly and the monkeys arrived and two weeks since the rest of the horses came back from the meadows in the south. Hope ... that's what was in the air, even stronger than the smoke which grew thicker every day. The horses hauled logs tirelessly, singing ancient, echoing songs only they could understand.

Courtland and his people were always smiling as they poured over the pictures and writings on the walls of Morningfeld. *Home!* The hope of finding it hung around them like a glow.

The monkeys seemed to always be joyful, even though their home was lost. It would be a long time until they could return. "We will make it even better, Growly!" Chippy would say, his mind swirling with ideas. "But first, we're helping the horses. Look how happy they are!"

The walkway was an astonishing construction, built according to plans Chippy had drawn up. Sturdy posts held the bridges and ramps, with ropes and spikes keeping it firmly in place. It zigzagged its way up the side of the cliff, and it wouldn't be long at all until they finally reached the top.

It was a relief to be almost there. Though everyone was hopeful, there was a sense of urgency.

Deep booms and rumbles echoed from the mountains to the south. Growly had ridden south a short way and had seen dark, black smoke belching out of the mountains. In Morningfeld, the smoke was growing thicker and thicker, and the water levels were rising in the lake next to the ruins. Staying in the Alps was becoming more dangerous everyday.

As they sat around a fire that night, Courtland was pointing excitedly to a map he had copied from a wall in the ruins. "Evon," he whispered, holding it close for Growly and Chippy to see. "I believe this could be the city of Evon … or *Evony!* It could be the place our ancestor's ship sailed from, the reason they called our village *West* Evony! To the east, that must be the way back home."

Chippy nodded excitedly, and Growly felt his heart leap with the adventure of unknown places. "On the Monkey Island you will find more answers. They have books and books and *more* books. Everything copied from the days of the Explorers. You could read them, Courtland. There will be answers there for sure. More maps to help you find your home."

Home. Growly felt an ache in his heart. Tomorrow or the next day, the platforms would be complete, and they would all leave these mountains and head out into the land between the Alps and The Precipice. They would say goodbye to Courtland and many of the monkeys who would travel with him to help the people of West Evony finish their boats. It would be a dangerous journey for them to the Endless Islands, but surely they would be ok. Surely they would be able to find their way. He could go home at last, to his village in the mountains, to his wonderful cottage, to his family, and to Ember.

Growly stood up and walked out into the dim moonlight. There was an awful, orange glow over the mountains to the south and on some of the peaks just beyond the lake. Growly shivered. What a strange time it was, of bears and monkeys and people all suddenly on the move. Hegel had written of such a time (though he had never known about monkeys or people). "Upside-down Days." It was a song he wrote on his journey. A funny song, which was strange, considering all he had lost.

My boots in the clouds,
And my hands in the grass,
I woke up this morning,
on a day that was dark.
But though I was lost,
I had home in my heart,
I had home in my heart,
And it all turned around.

On an upside-down day,
It was all turned around,
And the grass was the sky,
And the sky was the ground.
But though I was lost,

I had home in my heart,
I had home in my heart,
And it all turned around.

They had sung it, Hegel and the bears of his village, all the way across the wild. From a home they had lost, to a new one in the mountains.

30
Where the Ways Meet

long line of horses climbed slowly up the walkway, zig-zagging upward in small groups of two or three, so they wouldn't put too much weight on any one place all at once. The enormous, wooden structure creaked and groaned, but as the morning wore on, it held firm and strong.

After a group of twenty horses had made it to the top, the monkeys checked every rope and binding to make sure it was still secure. Then more horses would climb, coming up onto the cliff top with neighs and snorts of joy. No horse had seen this place, the narrow pathway out of the Alps, though they had imagined down through the centuries what it might be like. *The Way That Crevan Went* is what they called it. And through all the centuries since, how they wished that they could have followed.

"Mama!" Flurry whispered, turning in circles and stomping his hooves in the snow. "What will it be like, do you think? What will we see?"

Winterfrost smiled down at her son. She was just

as excited as he was and just as full of questions. What *would* it be like? And where would they go? Once they left their ancient home in the mountains, anything could be out there. It was frightening and exciting all at once. "We will see something new," she said with a gentle smile. "Something no horse has ever seen before."

"All here!" Chippy cried, as his head came up above the edge of the cliff top and he climbed up off of the walkway. Other monkeys were scrambling upward too, following the last few horses as they came onto the narrow plateau. There were hundreds of horses, stretching out through the valley and onto the stony trail which led up higher into the mountains. Storm, Whisper and Flurry's father and the leader of the herd, stood in the lead, calling out with a loud whinny, which echoed around them. Suddenly all the horses knelt down low upon the icy ground while the monkeys watched in astonishment. Whisper, who was still standing next to Growly, noticed the puzzled looks on their faces and let out a happy snort, which sounded almost like a laugh. She nudged Growly's arm and then knelt down next to him too, letting out another snort, and shaking her mane.

"They want us to ride!" Growly exclaimed, suddenly realizing what Whisper was trying to tell him. "Chippy! They want us to ride!"

Chippy's face lit up with a grin, and he called out to the monkeys around him, showing them how to slide up onto the horses' backs and how to hold on tight. Many of the monkeys looked very worried at first, but soon they were climbing on, with packs tied and arms clinging tightly.

The horses moved quickly up into the mountains, thundering along the narrow trail through the smoke and icy wind. Growly's teeth were gritted tightly, and his eyes stung from the murky haze, but the horses ran with confidence, neighing loudly to each other in the dimness, till they finally began to descend.

"The Northern Pass!" Growly shouted happily as they came around a final bend and out into the wide, open spaces. The horses, who had already been galloping very quickly as far as the monkeys were concerned, began to gallop even faster, neighing joyfully as they spread out over the gently sloping fields with monkeys, bear, and people clinging tightly on their backs.

"Fields!" Flurry cried. "Look mama! They go on forever!"

Chippy felt his heart leap with excitement as they sped out onto the grass. "Come on, Growly," he shouted, as Whisper raced by, carrying the wobbling bear onward as they sped through the herd.

"Lead the way!" Storm called to his daughter as they came up beside him. He shook his mane and looked up at Growly. "He will know the place to take us; we will follow as you carry him."

Growly knew it was time to lead them to The Precipice. That had been the plan. Once the horses were freed, they were to travel to The Precipice. It looked like they were going to get there a lot quicker than he was expecting.

"There!" he shouted, pointing straight ahead of them to the north.

Whisper nodded and let out another neigh, thundering out ahead of the herd as she led them over the grasslands. On through the afternoon they ran, the shadows of the horses and riders stretching longer as the afternoon wore on. The open fields turned to hills dotted with woods and rocky outcrops.

Coming out of a thick stretch of forest, Growly let out a gasp of surprise. There, just a few miles in front of them stood The Precipice, stretching upward and upward through the smoky haze, into the clouds high above. "The Great Falls!" Growly gasped, as he saw the torrent thundering down from the heights into an enormous lake which broke off into a network of rapids and rivers. Even from this distance, he could feel the damp chill of spray on the wind.

If this was the Great Falls then ... "That way!" Growly shouted, pointing out toward the east and waving to be sure that Whisper understood. The deep brown horse turned off to the right, picking up speed again as she raced onward down a slope and into another thicket of trees.

It was almost dusk when they came up to the towering cliff. The place was familiar, with a wide, grassy slope leading down toward a peaceful lake. And there, right down by the water, stood two tall, stone pillars.

"Growly!" Chippy cried. "We are here! And look!"

Chippy pointed out over the water to a cave, far on the other side.

"They did it!" he gasped. "The water is gone! Growly the water is gone!"

Growly was already off of Whisper's back, running as fast as he could on his aching legs down toward the water. They did it! The bears of Haven had managed to change the flow of the Cascade River and open the way back ... home.

Growly felt a strange, sudden ache in his heart as the thought came into his mind. He put the feeling aside again though, like he had been doing over and over for the last few weeks. He would know what to say when it came time to say it. Right now though ...

There was a sudden cry from the hillside and then loud cheers as a large group of monkeys came out of the forest.

"Meegwin!" Growly turned and ran back up the hillside to meet his old friend. Badru was with him too, and behind them, an enormous crowd of monkeys stretching back into the trees.

The elder monkey threw his arms around Growly, giving him a tight hug and then throwing an arm around Chippy's shoulders affectionately. "You did it!" he gasped. "Look at them! Magnificent!"

Badru was gazing up joyfully at Winterfrost. He had always loved birds and fish and all living things, but he had never seen anything at all quite like this.

"We've all come," Meegwin said seriously then.

"All of us from Towerwood. We were just going to bring a small group at first. To bid you farewell, Growly. And to welcome Annily when she arrived. But …"

Growly could see now the worry on the elder monkey's face. "What is it, Meegwin?" Growly whispered, leaning closer. "What has happened?"

"Growly, the Alps are full of fire now. We have to leave the Lower Lands!"

Growly looked anxiously around the clearing, and back at the endless line of monkeys and people coming up out of the forest. There were hundreds and hundreds of them, moving down toward the water and finding places on the grass. They were all exhausted, with mothers cradling their babies and little monkeys coughing from the smoky air.

"The smoke is everywhere now," Meegwin sighed in a worried voice, "and Towerwood is underwater. I don't know when we will be able to go back there again."

It was early morning when Growly heard it. He had been up by one of the signal fires, taking the last watch with Chippy in the hours just before dawn. There was a cry from the darkness, from out across the waters, where the dripping cave opened at the foot of The Precipice.

"Helloooo! Helloooooo!!!!"

The cry made Growly gasp, and Chippy blinked in wide eyed surprise.

"Ember?!"

Growly was off at a run, racing down through the camp site, leaping over bundles, and one or two sleeping monkeys, as he went.

"Ember! Emmmmber!" he cried, splashing out into the water with a happy laugh. The water was icy, but he didn't mind at all. With a kick of his boots he splashed out into the deep water, stroke after stroke until finally he reached the far shore.

"Ember!" he gasped again throwing his arms around her in a dripping, shivery hug.

"Growly!" Ember laughed, as she sniffled and wiped her eyes. Chippy was almost across the lake now too, and Growly and Ember cheered him onward, joined by other bears who were emerging from the cave.

There was a monkey with them also, bundled in a thick winter coat with the hood pulled up over her ears. She came up beside Ember, watching Chippy scramble up on to the rocks.

"Chippington!" Annily whispered, her voice crackly and croaky. Then she ran across the rocky ground and wrapped him in a hug.

31
Upside Down Days

Growly lay in the long grass by the Ocean, panting and trying to catch his breath after jogging all morning beside the horses of Morningfeld. It all seemed like a blur, the last week coming southward. The mothers and children from Courtland's village rode on the horses' backs, with Growly and a large group of monkeys jogging next to them.

Ember! The thought of her still left him with a deep ache, even though it would just be a month or so. Growly knew he had to help Courtland and the people of West Evony. Even though he felt Ember would agree it was what he should do, he was astonished when he heard her response.

"It seems we will both have our little adventures. You have to help them reach the Island of the Monkeys, and I have something else that I know I must do."

Something else!? Growly had listened with his eyes

wide as Ember told him of what had happened in the weeks since he left Haven.

"Balliwick returned from his journey to the ruins of Arborstone, to bring back supplies from what they had stored in the woods. One of the things he bought was a book, Growly. Some of the words copied from the caves in the far north. Words in People and, Growly, a few words in *Monkey!*"

There was not much Ember could have said that surprised him more than that.

"I'm going with them," Annily had whispered, giving Chippy a gentle smile. "To help them read the writings."

"Ember will need a friend like you," Chippy had finished. He knew how much help a good friend could be.

Rafts would carry the monkeys of Towerwood over the lake to the cave which led up into the Precipice. They would all go to the Upper Lands, for the summer at least, till the fires were over and the air clear again.

Many bears had come down from Haven to help, and soon the whole forest was alive with the sound of saws and hammering, and with laughter and songs. Never in the history of, well, history, had so many monkeys and so many bears been all in the same place, all at the same time. The bears had brought fresh bread and potatoes and apples, and every day of building ended in a glorious feast.

Then, after days which felt far too short for Growly, it came time to leave. The rafts ventured out onto the lake, and Growly and his companions bade everyone farewell. His father and mother, Meegwin, Merridy and C.J., and on and on. One by one, farewell after farewell, with many tears and hugs. "Just a month or so, Young Bear. We'll have watches set here each day." Just a month, but it was still hard to leave.

I lay and I watched,
As the wind whistled by,
And it lifted two wings,
That were waiting to fly.
And though it looked lost,
It had home in its heart,
It had home in its heart,
And it all turned around.

That verse of Hegel's song was about a bee of old that had led him eastward to the mountains. As Growly said his hardest goodbye, that verse had been buzzing around somewhere deep down in his heart, just like that ancient bee who was aching for home. And so he watched Ember and Annily disappear into the cavern, with a final wave as they went inside.

"Ready?!" Chippy's voice was loud and clear as he called out to the group. There were twenty of them from Towerwood: Barbod, Tappen, Jacory, and some of the young sailors who were ready for adventure. Courtland and the men of West Evony who had been with them at The Precipice had gone on ahead days ago, leaving Growly and the monkeys to bring every one else on the horses.

The Cove was just a short way ahead now. Growly could remember the rocky crags and thick bands of forest they were passing. Soon would come C.J.'s marker and the path down toward the shore.

They came around a bend and along a narrow stretch when suddenly Growly recognized the distant sound he had been hearing for a while now on the wind. Hammering!

"Look!" Chippy cried, pointing off into the trees to their left. It was C.J.'s rock, the one with his markings. And just beyond it, a clearing of stumps and trampled bushes led to the cliffs that looked down over the Cove.

There were boats out on the water—long, sleek, and polished with fluttering sails. "Monkey boats!" Chippy gasped, looking out over the fleet. There were more up on the beaches too. On and on and on.

"Chippy boats!" Barbod said, giving his friend a rare grin. All these boats had been built with the monkeys' help, following Chippy's designs. "We built most before the people went to Towerwood," Barbod explained. "Now, I think the men have finished."

The empty spaces in the Cove were filled with tents, and the ancient ruins had been made into workshops and shelters. It looked like a small city of white, with sails and coverings made from wide stretches of canvas. Men bustled to and fro in all directions, but when one of them saw the monkeys and the women and children up on the cliffs, there was a shout of utter joy.

The horses watched everything from a distance.

"Look at them all!" Flurry whispered to his mother, gazing out with wonder over the ships in the cove. There was a note of sadness in his voice as he asked the next question.

"Where will they go? All the people and their children?"

"To find their home again, I think," Winterfrost said softly. "Perhaps the same home Crevan and *his* people went to find."

"And what about *us* mama?" Flurry asked sadly. "Where will *we* go now?"

She was silent for a moment but then smiled as she looked down at her son.

"Wherever we want to," Winterfrost said, a spark of adventure in her eyes. "*Wherever* we want to!"

They left the next morning, Storm leading the herd with Winterfrost by his side. Flurry and Whisper were the last to leave. They stood next to Growly and

Chippy as the other horses started moving southward, nuzzling their friends for just a few moments longer. Chippy wrapped his arms tightly around Flurry's neck for a long time as he said his last goodbyes. Then, with a thundering of hooves and whinnies of farewell, Whisper and Flurry turned and took off after the herd.

It was just a few days later. With the last of the boats in place, the people of West Evony launched out into the harbor in silence, apart from the flapping and humming of the sails. Boat after boat made the turn around the headland, moving south for a short way before turning to the east, out into to the Ocean.

"Farewell," Courtland whispered, almost to himself, as he turned one last time toward the far off beaches of West Evony.

"Tack eastward to sea!" Barbod shouted over the waves. He was grinning from ear to ear as he stood high on the bow of the leading boat. A burst of spray flew up around him, and with happy howls of laughter the other monkey sailors let out a cheer.

"Chockle the Clove Hitch!" cried one.

"Flibble the Floorboards!" cried another. All of them were roaring with laughter now, mixing up the old sailing words and making up new ones as the coastlands fell behind them.

"Lubber the Line Log!" shouted Barbod, dripping and spluttering with laughter as another wave soaked him in spray.

Courtland turned back to Growly and Chippy, a smile getting bigger as the sadness began to fade.

"Can you feel it?" he asked, a look of wonder growing brighter and brighter on his face.

And as he looked out into the distance, Growly could suddenly feel it too. A warm gust of wind on the fresh Ocean breeze, like the first hint of spring at the end of the winter.

the end

the GROWLY books
Book 6
Sneak Peek

D isaster! We are three days ashore since the Willowwind went missing. Lost! Taken! And with it our supplies. They came, Durridge said, swimming silently through the water, while we were searching the caverns and caves in the cliffs of this astonishing island. And before he could raise the alarm, the sails filled full and the mighty ship lurched off, sailing out around the headland while he watched helplessly from the shore.

And so we have searched out around the eastern coast in the rowboats, till a heavy gale washed us far out into the surrounding sea and the island was lost, along with our ship. After two days in the storm, we came aground again here, a sheltered island cove amongst three towering peaks. We made camp on the beach, gathering food and stitching sails, to try and make for Sessawell before the winter sets in.

Growly looked over at Courtland, his eyes wide. "Sessawell!" he gasped. There was that name again.

"Yes, yes," Courtland whispered. "Just like in this book here. Look! This chapter is called The Sessawell Ledger, and right here …"

Growly stared at the markings at the top of the page. It all looked familiar, but he couldn't read a word.

"*Legend of the Willowwind.*"

Growly took in a deep breath, thinking for a long moment before he spoke.

"It might be in Sessawell then," Growly said slowly. "The clue could be in Sessawell. It must be the earliest of the People cities."

Courtland nodded excitedly again, pulling another book from a large pile on the table and opening it to a page they had looked at earlier.

"It's in *Histories*, Growly. Here on this page. '*To the foundation of Wesseren: Cadmus, Durridge and Carrigan.*' And then just down here, Growly. '*To the foundation of Athelstane, Madigan - Captain of the Willowwind.*'"

"Athelstane!" Growly exclaimed. "The captain of the Willowwind founded Athelstane!" Growly felt his heart suddenly sink. "Then it's gone! Everything is gone there, Courtland! We barely made it out of Athelstane before it was destroyed by rivers of fire. How will you ever find the maps you are looking for?"

Courtland smiled and patted Growly gently on his shoulder. "Athelstane *is* gone. But Madigan was in Sessawell first."

Just then there was a shout from the other side of the room, and Chippy came running over with another pile of books. "Sessawell!" he said excitedly in Bear. "Three times, and I think, even a map. Here! In the Endless Islands! I have seen that shape before."

Chippy ran over to an Elder monkey who was gathered with a few others around a long table at the end of the room. She was dressed a bright dress and an elegant coat, and there was a look of excitement in her eyes as they searched through the piles of books.

"Yamilet!" Chippy exclaimed loudly. He suddenly felt a little self-conscious in the stillness of the room.

The mayor's wife smiled warmly. She was just as excited as Chippy. Searching for clues in the history books made her heart leap with adventure.

"Sorry ... Yamilet ... look ... do you recognize this island?" Chippy was whispering again this time.

The Elder monkey looked at the map for a long moment, and then her eyes went wide as she saw it.

"Yes! Yes Chippy!" She hurried over to a wall of the long room, taking down a large framed map hanging above a bookshelf.

"There!" she said in excitement. "There, further to the east. That *must* be it. Look at that shape. That *must* be where the ruins of Sessawell can be found. No wonder the monkey cities south of us never found it. Look how many miles it is away."

"Sessawell," Courtland said in wonder, looking down at the island shape and the markings on the maps.

"Courtland!" There was a startled cry from across the room. Growly stood next to the far table, his eyes wide in shock, holding out an open book in his trembling paw.

"Courtland, read this please!"

They rushed over to Growly, Courtland taking the book from him and looking down at the page.

"Madigan!" he gasped in wonder. "It's part of a story I think."

Never such a place have I seen, jagged cliffs and tangled jungles rising up into the heights, thundering waterfalls and caverns, majestic mountains draped in cloud, and all about a still expectancy of something about to happen. We have anchored the Willowwind, and will venture out this morn'.

There were a few more pages then, talking about about other writings, fables, and mysteries. Growly had marked another place though, and as Courtland continued, he could see that it was another entry from Madigan's journal.

Strange sounds in the night, from far up in the mountains. Like booms of thunder or echoing voices in amongst the cliffs. Some men have seen shadows, or at least so they think. Up in the heights ... tall, they say ... like men ... but not. At first it was hard to believe, but then we found the cave. We are all afraid and will leave at first light.

Growly looked up at Courtland in alarm. With a

shaking paw he slowly turned the page of the book. As Chippy saw what was written there, he let out a cry of surprise.

Written at the top of the page were markings Madigan had copied from the cave.

"Bears!" Growly gasped, his voice trembly and shaky. "*Wild* Bears," he added, and he quickly shut the book.

About the Author

Philip Ulrich lives in South Carolina with his wife, Erin, their two daughters, and a Boingle.

He loves to spend time with his family and explore the beautiful Upstate South Carolina.

When he is not writing about bears, you can find him designing at www.philipulrichdesigns.com

Philip is currently at work on the continuing adventures of Growly.

About the Illustrator

Annie Barnett is a creative soul who spends her days making art, memories, and inevitably a good mess – whether it's with curry, paint, or play dough. She now plays house in the Hudson Valley, where she lives with her husband, three lovely daughters and an occasional pet ladybug. Her artwork can be seen at BeSmallStudios.com.